A
Boy
In
Winter

Other Books by Maxine Chernoff

FICTION

American Heaven

Signs of Devotion

Plain Grief

Bop

POETRY

Leap Year Day: New and Selected Poems

New Faces of 1952

Japan

Utopia TV Store

A
Boy
In
Winter

A   N O V E L

MAXINE CHERNOFF

CROWN PUBLISHERS • NEW YORK

Published by Crown Publishers, 201 East 50th Street, New York, New York 10022.
Member of the Crown Publishing Group.

Random House, Inc. New York, Toronto, London, Sydney, Auckland
www.randomhouse.com

CROWN is a trademark and the Crown colophon is a registered trademark of
Random House, Inc.

Design by Leonard Henderson
Printed in the United States of America
Library of Congress Cataloging-in-Publication Data

Chernoff, Maxine, 1952–
A boy in winter / Maxine Chernoff. — 1st ed.
I. Title.
PS3553.H356B69 1999
813'.54—dc21 99-20430
CIP

ISBN 0-609-60522-4
10 9 8 7 6 5 4 3 2 1
First Edition

For Koren, Julian, Philip, and Paul

Acknowledgments

With special thanks to Fred Shafer, Jim and Doris Stockwell, Tim Erbs, Marsha Berman, Robert Cornfield, and President Robert Corrigan and the College of Humanities of San Francisco State University for my Presidential Award semester leave.

Some of *A Boy in Winter* appeared in slightly different form in *Triquarterly* 104. My thanks to the editors.

"My heart tells me to stop right here."
—TIM O'BRIEN

Part One

Time

I REMEMBER THE face on the cover of *Time*. It was a British boy around ten years old, who had smothered a neighbor child while playing. I sat on my bed and stared at that cover. Danny was only two then, and his father had just left us. It took me forever to fall asleep in those days. My mind, like a spring tornado, spun with trouble. I focused on the boy's face until the page got grainy, and the photo looked crude, like a bad painting. Then I brushed my hair; it was still long—I suppose I wanted to look young—and wondered about evil, whether it's a force in nature or just in us.

I looked at Link, Alex's old dog, dumb gray animal panting up at me with eager eyes, and knew he couldn't be evil. I started pacing the room and looked down from the apartment window at the street where a single car was cruising like a phantom. Where was the driver going? Probably to meet a lover or to kill someone who had betrayed him, which is what I thought about often then. In my better moments I asked myself what weapon I would use to snuff out Alex when I found him. First I would confront him with all of the things I hadn't had the presence of mind to say when he left. I would walk back into his life like a Fury, my defense well-rehearsed, my vengeance a fine-honed instrument.

More often, I was up late, wanting Alex in bed with me, whatever the cost and humiliation, wanting him back so much that I could smell him in the air, hating him at the same time. It became a game I played. I conjured up his good side, which had held our son and made me laugh and touched me in all the right ways. Then I thought of the night he left, and how I was in a panic, unable to dismiss his face.

Alex smiled at me when he said he was leaving, like he was giving me a present. But my freedom wasn't a gift. I was still in love. And it wasn't freedom because he was walking away, and I had Danny. If that smile had meaning beyond a nervous gesture, I haven't stumbled upon it in nine years.

Then I went into Danny's room and held his hand. He was such a sound sleeper that unless I shouted in his ear, I couldn't have disturbed him. Holding on to him, I banished the thought that any child could do such a terrible thing. I wouldn't allow it to enter my mind or to occupy Danny's room with its shiny yellow walls and tulip-faced trim. When I went back to my bedroom, I threw the magazine away just like that.

Now that I'm looking for answers about Danny, I wish that I had saved it.

Slogans

I SEE CARS all the time with the slogan, "Guns don't kill, people do." I see cars all the time with the slogan, "When guns are outlawed, only outlaws will have guns." I see cars all the time with the slogan, "Shit happens," "Practice acts of random kindness," "Save the Whales." I want a bumper sticker that says "Save Danny." I need to understand, though, how it happened that I need to save him, how my son, a normal, eleven-year-old child, became newsworthy, how Frank Nova aided and abetted my son in this process, how a compound bow is fired, how it will feel if I lose Danny forever.

Sometimes I think being locked up with him would be the best solution. We could be sent away together somewhere safe. I'd still be able to take care of him then, and I could spend all the rest of my time figuring this out. What will Danny do in this new place, which I imagine to be Montana, woodsy and isolated, somewhere a boy can't meet other people and cause trouble? Watch TV, play video games, build model gliders, collect baseball cards, tell lame jokes that I pretend are funny, all the things he's always done: until we met the Novas and our lives changed, first for the better and then for the worse.

Social Science

MY MOTHER CALLED after she heard the news. She's a kind of hermit, she and her cats. I don't talk to her that often now that Dad isn't alive, which might make her feel inhibited with me. Instead, it makes her more frank, as if our estrangement is a way for her to leverage power when we do speak.

"I can understand those children at Cabrini-Green," she said, "doing things like this. They throw each other out of windows every day." Her voice was calm and low. I could see her in her housedress, coffee at the ready, a cloud of cats billowing around her ankles. "I can see why a child who has nothing, no love at all, goes out and harms another child. But Danny?"

I could only be silent, and my silence provided another window for my mother, who can jimmy any psychological lock. Knowing my mother's power to be fierce makes me believe in all those determined lady detectives that fiction is handing us lately.

"What did you do to him?" she asks flatly.

"Nothing. I love him, Mother."

"Did you sleep around? Did men visit you?"

"I had dates now and then, but nothing too serious."

I wasn't going to try and explain Frank Nova and me to my mother.

"There's always motivation, Nancy. Things make sense."

"Well, this breaks all the rules, Mom."

"Was he jealous of the other child?"

"Eddie was his friend. They were as close as brothers."

Then we didn't speak. She was probably pursing her lips and waiting for me to admit something. Give her some evidence; she'll grip it, jaws locked. While she waited for me to offer a guilty clue, the kitchen filled with the sound of order that intruded from outside. It was Thursday, and the streets were being swept. A giant whooshing engulfed the room.

"I've learned a lot from my cats, Nancy," her voice interrupted. "I can give you two examples. One cat I had, Chloe, the white one—you remember her maybe—was an only child. She was a crazy nervous little thing, afraid of her own shadow. And when she got too frightened, she'd sink her teeth into things. When we moved and Dad went to pick her up, she gave your father's hand a real good bite. Remember that?"

"I do."

"Well, I say it was being an only child."

More silence from me. No clues.

"The other possibility," she continued, undaunted by my silence, "is hardship. George, my new cat—you haven't met him—was a stray. He's the best hunter I've ever seen. Without claws he can pick birds right out of the trees."

"Amazing," I say flatly.

"We do what we need to survive."

"People aren't cats, Mother."

"I'm just saying that there was some need in Danny, some hole he had to fill."

"I still think he was playing. Without the bow, Eddie would be alive. This nightmare wouldn't be. I believe what he's told me. Why can't you?"

I think she said, "Wishful thinking, Nancy," before I hung up on her for the first time in thirty-eight years.

Life Opened Up

I REMEMBER THE day that Danny was born with great clarity. Even mothers rendered unconscious to relieve their pain have said this. I can't say that I haven't always been sentimental about it, but thinking of it now . . . his smallness against me, after he came out and rested on my chest, how it felt that first time he pulled at my breasts and they magically gave up what he needed. I had always prized my own intelligence, the ability I had to shape myself into a woman despite my mother, despite the fears that every girl has that the place inside her, her soul that should be, is somehow lacking. But as soon as I saw him, I began to trust my instincts; no one can try to convince me that it's reason that draws two people into a huddle from which heat and life grow.

This is it, I said when the birth waters gushed warm between my legs. And with every stab of pain, I repeated a vow: I will love and protect my child, I will never harm my boy. So many times I've broken this in small ways. Before this happened, I always felt that it was the first day of his life and that whatever went wrong yesterday—a nasty fall, an angry gaze, some faint shadow of disappointment temporarily skimming his face—could be corrected tomorrow. Life, I always thought, was a series of alterable scenes, an accordion of pos-sibility. I always imagined, and this is as close to religion as I ever got, that what connects us, what holds us all to this world is the river that flows from the moment that a life begins. The worst thing is losing that.

Solitude

WITH DANNY AWAY at the boy's facility for now, I'm alone for the first time since he was born. At work, I used to imagine what I'd do with any free time I might someday have. I saw myself getting pampered. I'd get a massage, a spa pedicure, meet Carol for lunch at a ferny place in a mall, buy some colored lights, those wispy Italian ones for the shaking trees outside the house. I could have done most of these things with Danny, of course, but it would have been different if I were alone, like someone's making a movie of me just for my winning smile and positive attitude.

I'd see films every day. I'd go to the bargain matinee and get the tallest Coke and the largest popcorn—with butter—and have it all to myself. I would sit up close, four rows back, right in the middle, and put my feet up, not worried about the example I was setting. I'd see all kinds of movies: not just my usual fare, the ones about women in trouble or in love or in both.

Now that I'm alone, I don't get massaged, pedicured, buy lights, see movies, or even talk much to Carol. I do my eight hours and come home. And then I call Danny and we talk, mostly small talk. His voice is so tiny that it frightens me. *The Boy Who Disappeared* I title the play that we're starring in, despite ourselves. I sit at the kitchen table and stare at the cabinets until their handles give off the sheen of a drug-induced dream.

Now I don't blink, and my eyes grow tired. I clear my mind except for one thought: Danny killed Eddie Nova. Sometimes I frame it in a thick black border. Sometimes I see it in red italics, the typography of emotion. The actual twenty letters: nine vowels, eleven consonants, three capital letters, three spaces. Seven syllables. The truth about my life, my son's life. A marquee, a headline, a pain so deep that I fall asleep with my head on a stack of mail and wake up with envelope creases on my cheek.

Do I cry? Every night. In the shower. On the phone with Carol.

Do I cry? Never at work.

Research

"What Your Child Needs"

1. Unconditional love mixed with respect.

2. Not just time—but your real presence.

3. Approval of your child just for who [s]he is.

4. Your loving insights to help your child understand himself.

—DR. T. BERRY BRAZELTON

The Romans introduced no important innovations with regard to missile weapons, learning all their techniques from the Carthaginians and Greeks. The bow commonly used in war (as with the Greeks earlier) was of the curved form . . . it was said to have been made from two goats' horns, fastened together at the roots in the central grip of the bow. But the straight bow was also known, since it is shown, for instance, in the hands of the gods.

The crossbow is described by Vegetius under the name manuballista *as the same weapon as that formerly called "scorpion."*

—HISTORY OF TECHNOLOGY, VOLUME 2

The crossbow was the leading weapon of the Middle Ages. The destructive power that made it so feared derived from the substitution of metal for wood in its construction.

The crossbow's merits have been demonstrated in modern times by sportsmen who have used it to hunt large game, although some jurisdictions forbid its use.

The bow was outlawed "at least for use against Christians" by the Lateran Council of 1139.
    —BRITANNICA MICROPAEDIA, 1990

10 Commitments for Parents
(8) I will encourage my child to experience the world and all its possibilities, guiding . . . [him] in its ways and taking pains to leave . . . [him] careful but not fearful.
    —FAMILY CIRCLE, FEBRUARY 1995

Punishment
It's imperative for serious juvenile offenders to know they will face a sanction. Too many of them don't understand what punishment means because they have been raised in a world with no understanding of reward and punishment.
    —JANET RENO, ATTORNEY GENERAL

A Sound

I FOUND DANNY under the porch stairs that night. When he heard my car pull up, he made a sound. It wasn't quite "Mom," and it wasn't quite a howl. It was an eerie combination of both, like he had unlearned how to speak.

"What is it?" I asked him. "Why are you in there?"

"Someone should give me the electric chair" is all Danny would say.

Inside, I found Eddie's body on our rug. He had already stopped bleeding.

Frank Nova

DANNY KNEW NOTHING about me and Frank Nova. Not that there was so much to know. Frank was handsome and helpful and nice to have around. He knew how water heaters and old furnaces and plumbing work. And Marilyn was nasty to him—right to his face like she had something to prove, so it must not have been very pleasant when they were alone, either.

Whenever he could, he'd come over and help me with things, especially when I first moved in, since there was so much to do in a fifty-year-old house that no one had kept up. That's why the house cost what it did—I'm a realist on the subject of money.

I'd make coffee and we'd sit around. He'd tell me about his work. Frank was a paramedic, and boy, did he see chaos everywhere. The things he saw aren't stories to be told they're so terrible, except the funny ones. People call ambulances for everything: headaches, hemorrhoids, hiccoughs. One woman called an ambulance for her collie. There was no telling what would end up in his van.

One day we were looking in his garage for some rope to use to move a sofa I'd found at a yard sale, a plump flowery thing that reminded me of a summer cottage my folks had once rented in Michigan. Frank kissed me, and I let him. A small friendly kiss, something to be hopeful about. After some time, we started talking on the phone from work. Now and then we met each other late at night. I guess Marilyn thought he was on duty. Or maybe she didn't care at all. I had a feeling things had gone sour for them a long time ago. That can happen to high school sweethearts. Frank wouldn't talk about it, though. He was still sentimental about Marilyn. When he mentioned her, he told stories that showed how proud he was: how, even with back labor, she had done Lamaze like a trooper, how she could beat him at tennis without trying. She was Frank's hero, so I'd guess the trouble had started with Marilyn.

I'd kiss Danny and tuck him in and make sure he was asleep. Then I'd meet Frank at a cozy Italian place for a Campari and soda. Joey's was named after no one we met, but it had a natty green and white awning and a laid-back atmosphere. It tickled Frank that I drank Campari since I'm Jewish and he's Italian. I told him how I'd noticed that in movies, Italians often play Jews and Jews Italians. "Like Ray Liotta in that movie about the little girl who wouldn't speak. A big Italian guy is called Manny in the movie."

"Maybe Jewish actors cost more," Frank laughed, and I rolled my eyes at him.

Once when Danny went to Carol's overnight, Frank stayed here. Even though it was June, the last day of school, we kept all the doors and windows shut. We were so nervous with Marilyn next door that we acted more like brother and sister, giggling in bed and making shadow puppets and using funny cartoon voices instead of our own cautious ones. Frank had a way of running his fingers through his hair, which was wonderful, thick and steely gray, like industrial smoke. He'd touch my hand and say my name a lot. With those blue eyes it was easy to fall for him, but he wasn't slick. This was a man who was trained to make people's hearts start again. He was good with his body, not afraid of intimacy. It was so natural for him that I don't think he had any idea how seductive it was. When it was almost morning and he had to go home, we finally made love. "Quick as bees," he smiled. Then he kissed me, showered, slammed his car door in the garage like he was just getting home from work, and walked into the house.

"It would be nice to have Frank for a father," Danny once said on the way to school as we passed all the usual places that were suddenly more vivid for his having said that: red red houses, blue blue sky. I wondered if he was checking out my reaction.

"He's a real good man," I told him. Sometimes I imagined Marilyn casting Frank out in a howling snowstorm. He'd come scratching at my door like my mother's dozen cats, and, of course, ears trained, I'd let him in.

No, I don't think Danny knew, and I don't think it would have mattered to Marilyn if she had. She was one of those women who hates things casually with great conviction. Once when I took her shopping (Marilyn rarely drove), she said, "I wish there was some way to have babies without having sex."

"I guess we could have ourselves pollinated like flowers."

"Anything," Marilyn said, "would be better than it is now."

"Are you unhappy with Frank?" I asked her. This was before Frank and I were more than friends.

"No, I'm unhappy with sex," she laughed. "I don't really need it. I work out like mad, Nancy. I take care of myself. I can make myself happy without anyone else getting involved." She was sitting there with her perfect posture and her little white shorts. Her legs were tan well into October, a real trick in Chicago. Even her face seemed to have well-developed muscles now that I examined it more closely. When she smiled at me, her teeth like little tiles, I tried to imagine her before she got so stuck on herself. She must have been a young cheerleader when she met Frank at some drab high school dance with the limp crepe paper decorations and the Kool-Aid punch bowl smeared with sherbet. They'd have made a beautiful couple way back then. Just as I was sitting there envying her long maroon fingernails and her lousy marriage, I heard her say just like that, "You can have Frank." We both laughed.

A few months later I took her up on the offer.

Eddie

WHAT CAN BE said about Eddie? He was a sweet little boy with Frank's pale-blue eyes and Marilyn's taut nervous body and gestures. I remember how he told me stories sometimes with so much exuberance that the words got confused. "Start again," I'd say, "and relax, kid." I remember how his cheeks would freckle up in summer. Redheads are prone to that. I remember him on our living room rug that terrible afternoon.

When a child dies you can't sum him up like an adult. That's the tragedy. What has he accomplished? Eddie learned to read at age six, Eddie loved to tell stories about monsters, Eddie had pale skin and a tough little body. He was built to last. I imagine Eddie lost in a forest and finding his way out. I imagine Eddie falling off a sailboat and managing to drag himself to shore. Some day Eddie would have made a good teacher or lawyer or president. Eddie was Jenny Rosemont's sweetheart in fourth grade. Eddie could be heard above the others on the playground. "His voice was like a bell," the choir director once told Frank. At the funeral, which I couldn't attend, Marilyn almost fainted and said his name repeatedly. Frank sat like a stone, Carol reported. Barely twenty degrees outside, it was hot inside the chapel, as if so much pain had created a new climate.

The priest said that here in America, where everything is technology, with dialysis machines and artificial hearts and human gene therapy, it's hard to imagine losing a child just like that. The priest, Riley said, offered no further consolation.

No one can get over it. Eddie's gone, they keep telling themselves.

And what am I to do with the rest of the sentence? Eddie's gone because of Danny. I see the two of them spinning into space, unhinged from this earth and its consolations; and the rest of us, left behind, like distant satellites flung out of orbit.

Eddie, I want to tell you that Danny loved you. He told me. And Danny wants you to know something else, too. He'd rather it had happened the other way. "Just you'd be sad the other way around, Mom," Danny told me. "That would have been better, maybe."

Because it wasn't a question, I had no answer. My mind, stiff with those words, deserted my body, which sat in its proper chair thinking it sad that I can count what I love on one hand.

A Day on the Job

CHILDREN TODAY TAKE forever to grow up. Carol's daughter Nan, a perfectly decent, bright kid, has finished a college degree with honors in history and French. She makes cappuccino out of a cart near the seals at the zoo and still lives at home with Mom.

Things were different when I was young. I got out of the house forever at eighteen and never thought of returning. I was able to get hired right away. I've made a living since I was twenty-two, which really helped when Alex left me with Danny. I wasn't one of those women who has to figure everything out from square one. But sometimes I wish I had the kind of job that kind of woman might get: I could flip pancakes or fold towels or string painted glass beads at the mall's hippie jewelry concession.

My line of work is so demanding because it requires that I be creative. I make greeting cards, not the messages but the graphics: blooming sunsets, overweight cats, cornucopia for Thanksgiving, ancient maps for bon voyage, silly-looking old men wearing party hats for significant birthdays. Even the standard lilies of the valley or voluptuous hearts fading into a cloud on a sympathy card require a good deal of faith.

When I sit in my cubicle unable to concentrate on anything

but Danny, I feel doubly pained: What can be said? And even if there were words and images for every circumstance, even the occasion of Danny and Eddie, they'd be inadequate. I, maker of inadequacies, am essentially a fraud. In my grimmer moods, I've sensed this but tried to dismiss its obvious truth.

I've discussed it with Carol, who usually agrees with my darker views, and with Nan, a sunny credulous girl, who is less predictable. This time, to be kind to their friend whose cheeks have grown permanent raccoon shadows, whose eyes are red and tear daily, they both objected. They collaborated on examples of the inauthentic, which included notorious government officials, past and present; showbiz hypocrites we all know and love; the coiner of the phrase "quality time"; the inventor of lawn flamingos; yuppies bowling. True, they made me laugh.

But I feel my fraudulence, and wonder, will I ever be happy enough to repress it again? Will life allow me this necessary treason?

Sundays

SUNDAYS WITH DANNY, my first impulse is to take his hand and run like hell. We're in the last scene of the movie where the rhapsodic music swells, the ocean glitters, the sun glows, and we walk away unscathed.

No, we're in a state-run juvenile home where authorities in blue coats are poking and prodding my son. How can the medical functionaries at Friendship House help Danny more than I can?

Ms. Riordan is talking to me. She's young enough to be someone I once baby-sat. Her lips are an unadulterated pink. She looks like she's worked here twelve minutes. "Danny is suicidally depressed," she explains.

"Of course, he shot someone. Wouldn't you be, too?" I can feel my face take on color, see spit fly from my imperfect lips. I'm a rabid dog. I'm her worst nightmare. But apparently, I'm no original. There's a location on Ms. Riordan, M.S.W.'s chart, for my attitude. All of my rage at her idiocy is grist for their familial symptom mill.

Remember yourself, I say in my mother's most strident tone. *Breathe evenly. Visualize. Count to ten,* I remind myself, as Carol would in her best yoga voice. Then my practical wisdom rises to the surface: *Save it for the lawyer. You can call him on Monday. Don't let them think you're a bad mother. Don't let them take Danny away.*

Danny and I haven't seen Alex since he grew a beard and a new family three years ago. They are named Karina and Lilith. Lilith is the child. This Sunday, the third that Danny's been away, Alex is joining me for the visit. Meeting him at Friendship House is either a new beginning or the final turn of the screw. Carol calls his sudden interest in Danny Alex's coming-of-age. Nine years late, I say. Thirty-nine years late, she corrects me.

When I see Alex down the hall, I can feel my eyes well over. I turn toward the wall and chew on my lip, a substantial enough piece of myself to remind me not to cry. Not in front of him, I tell myself. Not now.

"Alex," I say, recomposed, leak-free.

"Nancy," he smiles, the same Mona Lisa shadow of a grin that he offered up the night he left. "How's Danny doing?"

"What do you expect? He's distraught. He's beside himself."

"You mean he understands?"

"Of course he understands. Didn't you listen at the hearing? He understands perfectly."

"I mean, it's got to be tough."

"It is tough."

"Well, often when things are hard we try to forget them."

"Alex, they're holding him here. He's a prisoner until the judge decides he can go. What do you imagine he'd think about in his spare time? They're wiping his face in it."

"Keep your voice down."

"It is down. Do you want to hear me raise it?"

"Nancy, I don't want to argue. I just want to see Daniel."

Daniel, a word he has no right to utter, a forbidden word, the name we gave to the product of our temporary commitment.

"Then I'd suggest we stop talking and walk through that glass door. Before you go in, though, you should know that he may not be all that delighted to see you. I think he'd like to crawl in a hole and die at this point. He's not much for big hellos."

"I can handle that," Alex says, his voice fracturing with nervousness.

"It could break your heart, Alex. I want you to know that."

"You seem to be dealing with it."

"I fall apart daily."

"Then the legend isn't true?"

"What legend?"

"You're a woman of steel. You can take anything."

"What gave you that idea?"

"When I called . . ."

". . . and I said I didn't need your help? You misinterpreted me. I'm ready to fall apart but not for you, not by you, not on you."

"Do people fall apart on cue, like it's a show they can perform or cancel?"

"Alex, you've always been smug with me. Even when you left me with Danny you were smug about it, God knows why. I'm not about to have you pull emotional rank over this. I've been with this child for eleven years. Where in the fuck were you?"

The nurse presses a button and we enter the locked wing of Friendship House, Pavilion Five.

Danny doesn't know what to make of the odd fact we're together. On days I can see him, I'm not allowed to call, so I've had no way to prepare him for Alex's visit.

"Hi, Mom," he says in a small, hopeful voice. "Hi, Dad."

I take Danny's hand and feel him lurch toward me with such momentum that I wonder if I'll manage to stay anchored. "Honey, you look okay," I whisper.

"I am okay," I hear him say from where he's buried his head somewhere inside my shoulder. Danny is one inch taller than I am. To regress into me requires that he stoop over and slouch.

"Well," Alex says. "How about a hello for me?"

"Hello," Danny says and extends his hand for a Mr. Schulien handshake. We can learn so much from lawyers, I think to myself.

"How about a hug?"

"Okay," Danny says, waiting for Alex to begin.

Fishing

THE SUMMER BEFORE he taught them to use the compound bow, Frank took Danny and Eddie fishing a couple of times. The first time both boys acted badly, and they came home early. So Frank approached the following trips like expeditions. They planned the weekends with the care of a moonwalk. They took notes and read guidebooks and even practiced setting up the tent in Eddie's yard. It was a big deal for Danny, being away from home and "doing boy things," as we jokingly called it. Until we moved next door to Frank, we were so distant from these activities, Danny and his well-meaning female entourage of mother and friends, that "doing boy things" came to connote the special effort it took, fatherless, to engage ourselves seriously enough to convince Danny of our seriousness. Doing boy things meant Little League baseball. Danny was one of the few kids who couldn't throw right when the season began. "Don't throw like a girl," one memorable coach remarked. Doing boy things meant letting Danny get a skateboard that led to altering the length of his two front teeth on an unexpected curb. It meant riding his bike more than a mile to school before spring had displayed its first green shoots under the snow. I bought Danny his own lantern and sleeping bag for the trip. For window dressing, I threw in a Swiss army knife, a red bandanna, and an army surplus camouflage canteen.

From all reports, the trip went well. I can show you photos of the tall dark pines and Fuji film–azure sky at Kettle Moraine State Park. Bluegill sizzle on a miniature red grill as Danny and Eddie stand side by side, buddies forever. But there's one photo that concerns me. Danny took it at Frank's request. It shows Eddie and Frank together, only the odd thing is that Eddie's hardly in it. Standing on a gray, sloped rock, Frank is at the center of the picture. Eddie is leaning out of it, so that part of his face and body are missing.

Now, Danny knows how to take pictures. That's one advantage he's had in life. Most boys without fathers can aim a hammer or a camera with some skill. So I have to wonder—did Danny arrange this excision? Should I show anyone?

My heart pounds as my search for clues leads me to his yellow, embossed baby book, where I read, "Danny is a jealous little boy. When he sees Alex kiss me, he tugs at my face."

Me, a word larger than its two meager letters. *Me. Me. Me,* a billboard blinking endlessly into the night. *Hold me, thrill me, kiss me,* the ballad demands. Our children's needs should be the subject of love songs—they're so much stronger than any other human requirements.

Reading the Obits

EVERY MORNING I open the paper and turn to the obituaries. I've noticed that some papers, the *New York Times,* for instance, are more likely to print the cause of death than others. Some papers, I'm sorry to say, don't even print the age of the person who died. But I'm specializing as I read. I'm looking for the obituaries of children. Many seem to die from cancer and heart ailments, those who die of diseases. I can imagine the shallow breathing required to resign yourself to that eventuality. But I'm more interested in the lives that are taken; the occasional drowning, the car crashes, the self-inflicted wounds that get reported as the pack heads toward their teens. I don't know what I hope to find. Maybe I'm looking for Eddie's twin, another child ripped from life by someone's mistake. I think if I found such a report I'd weep for joy just to know that Danny's not alone in the world.

But I come across other things, too. In a town near San Francisco, a man shot his head off trying to kill a woodpecker in his yard. In Phoenix five died when a car jumped the curb. Both of these happened in one day. And I wonder what else happened on the day that Danny killed Eddie. Maybe it was an especially awful day in the world. Maybe it held only the usual chaos.

Guy

THE DOG IS my best insomniac companion. Sometimes it isn't clear who decides that we need to practice this somnambulistic routine. We look into each other's bleary, sad eyes and take off into the night.

Last Sunday when I came home from visiting Danny, I took Guy out after midnight. The sky was a dark bowl, but we have these fancy alleys on Elmdale, better than the streets of some towns. They're all paved and brightly lit by the neighborhood association, which also plants marigolds on corners and shovels old people out in winter. On a moonless night like this, it's bright as Christmas behind my garage.

I heard a rustling behind me right between our house and Frank's. I turned around, actually whirled on my heels, but saw nothing. I felt queasy then and nightmare scared, as if my anxieties about Danny had created a presence in the world that could approach me with a body and a will of its own. All those frightening movies I wouldn't let Danny watch work on that same principle. Now, my own dark thoughts make me imagine evil everywhere, lurking in alleys.

Is good the opposite of evil? A TV minister asked that a few nights ago before I caught his larger drift. (I have an overactive trigger finger on the remote now that it's my job. First it was

Alex's, then mine, then Danny's, now mine again.) No, *hope* is the opposite of evil, I told Carol the other day. She hadn't asked, but I was thinking about whether I can hope for anything.

Poor Guy. He doesn't care about philosophy. My ideas are as important to him as roses or tea cozies. But Guy's a thinker, too, and an optimist at that. As soon as I took him back inside, he acted as if I had never let him out. He stood by the door and cried and whined, but I wasn't about to go into that alley again. I opened the door to the yard and watched from the back window, absentmindedly, until my eyes fixed on someone in a dark parka near the trash cans in Frank's yard. Marilyn was walking back and forth to her garage. It looked like she was cleaning house, only it was now one in the morning.

I don't blame her for wanting to leave, if that's what she's planning to do. I can't sleep in this house with Danny away temporarily. I don't think I could stay one night if Danny were gone forever.

That's my hope, I told myself, that Danny's coming back to me. That our lives will resume in some fashion. That this house will hold the noise of my child.

I stood at the door and called to Guy softly. He had taken to barking at Marilyn by now as she went back and forth so deliberately with her formidable boxes and lampshades and brooms. When I began wondering why Frank wasn't helping Marilyn do whatever she was doing, I understood.

I used to fear Frank leaving before this all happened. Marilyn would do something that would make him disappear forever. I knew if that happened, it wouldn't be within my power to change it. My life was contingent on Marilyn, who kept Frank next door on terms only they grasped. There was a shaky equilibrium as Frank spun between our two houses.

Sometimes I hated myself for being kind to Marilyn, as a way to maintain this delicate arrangement. I soothed her when she appeared perilously upset with him and offered to do her little favors to keep her appeased. What kind of maniac was I to take her shopping and listen to her complaints and agree with her about the foibles of men? Often our conversations took an odd turn. Someone monitoring them might have thought we were discussing a breed of dog, whose lineage had been flawed through excessive inbreeding: "Yes, they do have trouble concentrating." "I know what you mean about the upper lip. Alex used to bare his teeth when he was irritated, too." "You're right. They never remember what we say from day to day."

Since my life without a companion could have resumed at any point—my echoless voice in the bed, my one pillow, my towel—all of the things that thrive in pairs would disturb me with their presence whenever I imagined Frank going away. Sometimes when I was clumsy and broke a wineglass, I wondered if it wasn't an omen that I'd be alone again soon.

So I became watchful. Maybe you'd call it obsessed with little things. I'd check Frank's driveway. If his car was gone, I'd untense my muscles only when I heard his tires on the asphalt. On my walks with Guy, I'd peer into his trash, for what I didn't know. Once when he left a sweater here, I didn't return it but gave it its own drawer, a secret shrine.

Frank was more than a distraction to me. Once, when he called me by her name, I asked if he ever made the opposite mistake at home. He gave me such a curious look that I knew I didn't need an answer. The moment passed because there aren't words for the situation in which you find that your lover doesn't mirror your passion but can only diminish it. It was natural that I would care more since I had nothing to lose.

Aren't most martyrs and fanatics desperate people without proper human attachments? Who would consent to be burned at the stake if there was a table set and a proper dinner prepared and a pillow awaiting the distinct impression of our mortal heads? We burn for love, but we only consent to being burned in its absence.

I realize that I hardly think about him lately. True, I have another cause and, true, I'd wear a hairshirt, walk on nails, or poke out my eyes to get Danny back.

Still, faced with Marilyn's figure in the garage, I think of what I can save. I could warn Frank that she's planning to go and he could race home. I think of calling Frank at the station. A man so good at saving lives would want to stop this hemorrhage at home. I could leave a message for him without identifying myself. Thinking of punching the numbers, my pulse races like a teenager's.

But what right do I have to any part of his life, even the slippage? Danny has disqualified me. Would I feel this way if Frank and I hadn't made love, if his lips hadn't breathed words in my bed? Fingerprints would reveal all the things he's touched here. DNA tests might show him on my sheets and my towels and inside of me.

I've taken to doodling now, which is what insane people do in their spare time. It's better than cleaning out my refrigerator, which now contains a quart of milk past its date, three Granny Smith apples, and half a cooked chicken. Angry women are spartans; they also have the cleanest refrigerators. On the little diagram I've drawn, Frank and I are dots that can't be connected because of the pain. But the body gets lonely remembering, and the pain hovers like a cloud over our two houses. Will it ever blow away, or will we breathe its anxious air forever?

The phone rings and I pick it up, adrenaline running like a train through my veins and chugging in my head. When nobody talks, I hang up. I sit up in bed and look around. Everything's in place. There's no reason for me to enumerate the objects—chair, TV, nightstand—in the soft light of my room but to calm myself. Guy comes over to me and lays his long-jawed bullet head on my lap. We breathe together in the uneasy darkness, and he whimpers like he knows something about sadness. I'm wondering about the call when the phone rings again.

"Mom, it's me," Danny's voice whispers.

"What is it, honey?"

"I just wanted to say hi."

"Where are you calling from?"

"It's like a nurse's station."

"And where's the nurse?"

"She's asleep."

"That's why you're whispering?"

"Right." We both laugh.

"Say hi to Guy."

Guy tilts his head at Danny's voice, which could be transmitted from outer space for all my ability to have him with me now.

"I wish you were home with me," I whisper back, caught in the mood.

"Me, too," Danny says, a short sob stopping his words.

We sit like this, breathing into each other's ears for at least another minute before I interrupt. "Listen, honey. Go back to your room now, and get some sleep."

"Talk to you tomorrow, Mom."

"Did you call before, Danny?" I ask quickly, but he's already hanging up.

As soon as we finish talking, the phone rings. I pick it up. Silence again. Without much thought, I run to my kitchen window. I can see Marilyn in her kitchen by her sink. I'm unable to tell if she's using the phone.

Earlier this evening was the first time I'd seen Marilyn since Eddie was killed. Maybe she wants to talk to me. One of the worst results of all this is that people who share the same fate can't discuss it. I thought of going to the funeral, but everyone supposed I shouldn't, and when I started dressing to go . . . well, that's another story.

I resolve to call Marilyn in the morning if she's still around.

Weddings and Funerals

I WAS SITTING in my mother's living room wearing black because my father had just died. Danny was thirteen months old and crawled around the mourners' ankles. As a joke (yes, babies make jokes—don't tell me otherwise), he started sucking on my calf. *Ba ba,* he said, and I produced the punch line, his object of adoration, with its measured dose of two percent milk.

"Why did you stop nursing him?" my mother asked.

"Because it's too hard to do that and get to work on time," I muttered.

But my mother didn't care what I said, nor was she interested in knowing my opinions on any subject. She had made that clear forever. Even when I was little she shushed my simple questions.

She wasn't distracted by her grief but rather buoyed by it. My father had been ill for a long time. It was her day of release, this time of mourning for him. Because it happened just before Rosh Hashanah, there wouldn't be a week of it. This was the one day she got to show the world how she felt. And how she felt, I'd say, was pretty swell. She put cream cheese on a bagel and lined some olives up on her plate. She made sure, by positioning herself near the door, that every visitor saw her in her prime: my mother, an attractive woman with a square body and not an ounce of compassion, taking it all in from the couch. It was the same place where my father had faded for years, his "sick bay," he called it, where his bones became chickeny and his face took on a mocking boyish thinness that wasting diseases dispense to their hosts. She and Alex boldly shared the bay window, a stage where they'd reclaimed the world for the healthy and the strong.

I let Aunt Sheila, who had never had children, who spent most of her life "a single lady," she said with a catch of a question in her voice as if she could hardly believe it herself, hold Danny. He squirmed and pulled away, exhibiting the range of his vocabulary: *Mama up mama up.* He chained the syllables together and insisted that Aunt Sheila's arms remain empty. And I looked at his pink insistence, his good-natured egotism, and thought that this was the bud of the splendid boy that my father would never know.

Aunt Sheila was telling me her favorite story, VE Day, the Champs-Élysées. She was a nurse with brassy red hair and lips so red that they left a mark on the boys she kissed on the street—white ones, black ones, skinny ones, French ones. All the soldiers in sight had benefited. "But now," she said with a jauntiness covering her regret, "I haven't kissed a man in—what?—thirty years." She rolled her eyes and let out a horsey bray, then placed a hand over her mouth in contrite respect for her brother-in-law's passing. "He was a prince, Nancy."

"I know."

"To stay with your mother, God help him, he was a prince," she whispered.

"You can kiss me," Alex interrupted, and Sheila blushed.

"Don't sneak up on us like that!" she scolded, waving him off with her busy fingers.

I shook my head and took a big smoke-filled breath. Uncle Max, Mother's oldest brother, still smoked cigars. He'd lit one near the lazy Susan, but no one would object today. It was like a party at my mother's house because my father, who had taken seven years to die, had finally given up the fight. "At least he's not suffering," my mother offered to the guests, who agreed with nods and murmurs and more prune danish and decaf and strawberries dipped in brown sugar.

And she was right about suffering. When we die it stops. But I was sitting there in my little black skirt and jacket thinking something else. For so many years, even before Dad had gotten ill, they had suffered each other's presence. It was a well-known fact. And just like them, steering their little boats into constantly troubled water, Alex and I were having a war of our own. Before we had arrived at my mother's, we had at least six skirmishes. From the moment we had gotten up the morning of my father's funeral, we had exchanged words, light artillery that finally did more damage than its meager firepower. If babies remember their infancy, Danny wouldn't think of the geometric mobiles and little ducks on his blanket trim but of snarling, raised voices: the ballistics of anger.

I remembered Carol telling me that it was her husband's father's funeral that had gotten Bill thinking: "I'm forty years old and I'm just like him." A few months later, Carol and Bill had decided that marriage counseling couldn't help. Maybe there's something about funerals that provides more outline to every moment. Maybe the scales we use to weigh up experience get balanced at these events.

Weddings serve a different purpose, akin to parades and holidays whose significance we've forgotten. I remembered the infectious strains of "Moon River" at his boss's wedding reception softening Alex's regard for me only weeks before he left. "You look beautiful," he told his limp-haired wife as he cupped his hands around her behind and ever so delicately massaged her reluctant back. *He's touching me like he loves me,* I heard my confused self repeating.

Nearly a year before Alex left, I sat at my father's funeral thinking two things: that kind men shouldn't die. Keats's immortal vase should hold us all at our best moments: me, suspended on the rope swing my father had fashioned, his capable hands lifting me into the sky; Aunt Sheila locked in an embrace with some huge soldier from the Dordogne; Alex, just when he met me in European history class and shot me a smile that had nothing in common with a sneer. My ode to immortality was interrupted by my knowledge of impermanence. *Alex and I won't last. Alex and I won't last,* I chanted to myself like Danny's invocation of his beloved bottle. When Alex touched me at the wedding, it wasn't an initiation. It was part of the denouement.

The day Eddie was buried I lost control. I asked Aunt Sheila to take Danny because Carol wanted to go to the funeral, and I had hoped to go with her. But when the morning came, I knew I couldn't abide the pained decorum of the event, or worse, the hysterical release of emotions that might ensue. But Carol, who had known Marilyn and Frank from neighborhood activities for years, felt an obligation. I reassured her that I was fine, but when she hung up, I took out a bottle of scotch who knows how old; that's how often I drink. It was probably left over from Alex a decade ago. I began civilized enough, pouring a knuckle of it over ice, but by eleven A.M., when mass was to be said at St. Gregory's, I was pouring whole cupfuls, and downing them like a sailor. Choking on tears and rocking on the ground holding the bottle to my lips, I polished it off like air. I was saying *Eddie Eddie Eddie,* crying all over Guy, who loves occasions like this. Human tears are balm to him. He watched me patiently as I took out a bread knife and held it to my wrist, where a steady pulse throbbed in my drunkenness, where I could never cut.

At seven that night, when Carol couldn't get me on the phone and Aunt Sheila didn't know what to do with Danny after kids' shows had ended and dinner was served, I was found unconscious on the floor still holding the knife. Carol's friend Riley, who works for the IRS, got the locksmith to break open the door. Lying in my black suit, the one I had worn to my father's funeral, I was covered in dog hair, vomit, and tears.

They helped me shower and gave me coffee and water and fresh air. Danny spent the night with Aunt Sheila. "I haven't had a man over all night for four decades," she told me on the phone the next morning.

Note

SOMETIMES I PICTURE my life as a greeting card, the kind that unfolds to reveal scene after scene and costs $3.75. Scene One: My mother, a vampirish-looking new bride in very dark lipstick, is swaggering down Michigan Avenue with my father, who is a sailor. It is World War II and everyone is happy.

Scene Two: My mother miscarries. She is sitting in the window with her arms empty. Her face is framed in too-bright light.

Scene Three: I am born a decade later to two aging parents who no longer get along. Even in photos of my first few months on Earth, we all look like refugees from a country in turmoil.

Scene Four: The daughter of the vampirish mother gets married. It is a small ceremony attended by latter-day hippies. No one knows the proper gift to bring or the correct attire. One friend is photographed wearing a pair of denim shorts and striped knee socks. The newlyweds look mildly dazed or giddy with pleasure. In the typical cake-sharing photo, there seems to have been an earlier disaster. The cake looks uneven, disheveled, like a hat that has seen better days. The bride and groom kiss, their eyes floating like candles in water, full of hope and impermanence.

Scene Five: A baby is born to the young couple shown in Scene Four. He is wide-eyed with a moon-face. He is the prettiest baby they have ever seen.

Scene Six: The father is leaving in a beige sedan. No one is waving. The baby has all his teeth and can say words. This isn't a photograph but an air-brushed drawing. The baby has a speech bubble over his head. He is saying, "Bye, Daddy." The mother, who looks sullen, has a speech bubble over her head. She is saying, "What took you so long?" to the shadow of the moving car.

Scene Seven: The mother and son move into a new house and live happily ever after. The story, despite its dubious record of success, ends there.

Toys

WOMEN ARE DESPERATE in so many ways. You're Aunt Sheila and your life, rich with good female friends and art films and high premium museum memberships and worthy political causes, deflates to a joke about celibacy. You're my mother, a frustrated businesswoman, whose only real job was managing my father's death. You're Carol, hooked to fat Riley Flowers, Riley of golf and green for St. Patrick's Day and so little imagination that you congratulate him for remembering a dream. You're me, in bed with Frank, not uttering a protest when he tells me he's taking Danny deer hunting for the weekend.

Danny, who had to bite or tear pieces of toast into gun shapes because I refused to buy him a toy weapon. "Your gun has jelly on it!" I'd say and Danny would usually laugh. Danny, who fashioned shivs from aluminum foil for his backyard games of pirate.

"What's wrong with you, Frank?" I should have asked. "What are you thinking? Why do boys need to learn this in a world where warfare is conducted by electronic mail between attorneys? Why not take him to divorce court if you want him to be a man? Frank, why does Danny need to learn to kill anything?"

But I was in bed with Frank when he first brought it up.

Imagine a man and woman naked, a nipple sucked red, dried semen on the man's furry belly, all the exhaustion and camaraderie of good sex perfuming the air. "I want to take your son for a weekend in the woods," the man says. He has just given the woman such great satisfaction that her body is still vibrating with it. If she could see her own face, she'd notice a warm blush washing this portrait of her surrender.

"A weekend in the woods," the woman says. "But can't you just fish?"

"It's too late in the season to fish. We'll hunt," the man smiles.

Hunting, the drowsy woman thinks. And without a word she turns her face away from the issue toward the window where the afternoon sun, through the rice paper shade, is a game intruder.

The Movie Version

A MR. WOTOCKI from HBO is on the phone. He is offering to pay all of my legal expenses if I'll cooperate with him on a film about Danny and Eddie that would start with their friendship and "take it from there."

"Take it from where?" my incredulity responds.

"The whole story," Mr. Wotocki explains.

"How did you get my number?"

"From an Alex Horvath."

"Please leave me alone."

"But Mrs. Horvath . . ."

"I already have a lawyer. I don't need your money."

"I just want to give you a chance," he says, and I wait for more. My mother's phone torture has tutored me in the game of silence, which can be taken for firmness by the caller, who can't see my fingers fumbling with kitchen trash: potato peelers, matches, wire cutters, the small arsenal I've found in my drawer.

"We can make it without you, too," he continues. "This is a fictionalization, Mrs. Horvath. I'm just trying to involve you in the project to help you out."

"How can this possibly help me?" I ask, ears alert, mouth tasting the furious juice my body is manufacturing to protest.

"Well, a Mrs. Nova . . ." He pauses and I take the bait.

"Yes?" I gulp urgently.

"Mrs. Nova has already agreed to work with us on the project. I just thought you'd like to see your side represented, too."

The phone is in its cradle, where I must have slammed it, and I'm dialing her number.

When Mrs. Nova doesn't answer, I find myself outside, coatless and barefoot, beating on her door. This must go on for some time because later, staring at my knuckles, I see that they've sprouted purple bruises and shed some skin.

Maybe the State is right to have taken Danny away. Maybe it's for his protection from this howling creature, this modern-day mother of Grendel, who is standing on the steps shouting Marilyn's name to the late-afternoon moon, which peeks through a tear in a cloud.

I stare at my toes, naked in March, and think how this could be a scene in the movie version.

When Irish Eyes Are Smiling

BECAUSE IT'S ST. Patrick's Day, and because my lawyer, Schulien, whose name must mean "relative of the tortoise," cares nothing about Mr. Witocki and HBO, I'm sitting with Carol and Riley at the Glendale Inn. Mid-March should mean the beginning of spring, but the air is agitated and the lake a sinister gray. Maybe it'll stay winter forever, I thought on the way here. I've bundled myself into a black velour sheath. From my neck to above my feet, which sport black Keds, I'm dressy. Carol, always tasteful in dark woolly tweeds, is smiling benignly at Riley, her overripe leprechaun, when I approach their table. Despite the temperature outside, which hovers at twenty degrees, Riley glistens with sweat and expectation because it's his favorite night of the year. It won't take much to get him onstage at this neighborhood Irish bar and terrible restaurant with karaoke on weekends and holidays.

Because I decided on the day of Eddie's funeral that I'd might as well drink—what am I saving my sober self for?—I've had three shots of Bushmills and toasted everyone in sight: Carol, for always being there; Riley, for picking me off the floor the day of Eddie's funeral; the Chicago police, for patrolling my block during recent emergencies including my own; Mayor Daley, who, despite his poor locution, lets people like Danny and me live in his jurisdiction.

Now, onstage, a woman has begun mouthing the words of a recording of John MacCormack's distant stringy tenor, "Dear Mother of Mine." A round lady in a flowered housedress and thick support hose, her steely curls wobble and bounce as her heavy voice combines with the chorus now and then, breaking karaoke rule number one, never let yourself be heard for too long. I'd read that at a tough bar in the Bronx, a man was shot for taking this same liberty with his karaoke solo. His voice rising heedlessly over the soundtrack of the song, another zealous drunk silenced it forever. (Why do these stories of absurd motives still make me smile?)

But here we're more forgiving. As the woman's cheeks float like peach halves in the smeared reflection of the glittery green and yellow lights they've strung for the evening, the crowd cheers for her, a mother on Saint Patrick's Day. Surely St. Patrick, killer of snakes, domesticator of Ireland, the prime mover of our current celebration, had a mother somewhere in a low stone barracks among some ancient shrubs. She was proud of her son's missionary fervor, as mothers are always proud of their sons.

And now I notice that Carol is watching my face and maybe following my thoughts though she can't imagine where they've swerved. Her rapt interest creates tension for the next moment when big tears form in my eyes and my face begins to slowly crack around the mouth. "Danny is an Irish name," I tell her. "Oh Danny, Boy, Oh Danny Boy, I love you so," I hum, without saying a word.

"It's okay," Carol is saying, "to cry your eyes out, hon."

"It's okay, Nancy," Riley Flowers's mouth intones over his garish green turtleneck and under his silly Irish cap.

And because they're all staring at me, because I hate to cry on a holiday that isn't even mine, I remember the opposite side of the Emerald Isle; looking toward England, I keep a stiff upper lip.

The Cheese Stands Alone

AFTER I'VE DRUNK too much at the inn and admired Riley's impassioned, off-season version of "Auld Lang Syne," I hug my friends good-bye in the sharp cold and think how itchy it must be for Riley to kiss Carol, swathed in wool like an infant, and how wet it must be for Carol to kiss Riley, bathed in sweat like a runner. Then I come home and lie on my couch, listening to my pulse assigning me the present and future. If I never moved again, if, for some reason short of death, the moment were to continue, I'd be host to this internal chorus. Since time has become uniformly sad, the drumming ears and refrigerator hum and wedge of street noise might appease me forever.

Last spring Frank and I ventured out of the neighborhood to celebrate St. Patty's Day, the perfect holiday for an Italian and a Jew to surreptitiously share. We went to North Avenue, and at the River Shannon, an upscale bar with remnants of green from its life before gentrification, sat in a tight dark booth. That was the night Frank suddenly cried and renounced me as a penance. "It has to be this way, Nancy." He pushed my pain lever to the floor. "I love you too much," he said in a halting whisper perceived as a deep sickness in my chest. At times like that I have always thought of Danny, my anchor of sense. *I have Danny* were the words I carried as a banner of reason against Frank's periodic abstinence.

"What, giving me up for Lent?" I asked quietly without provoking a smile.

It was only a week before Marilyn went too far and drove Frank toward me again. "What is it this time?" I asked my contrite suitor.

"She's planning a vacation," his stunned voice confessed. "She and the kids are going away without me."

"Too bad we can't see each other anymore now that you'll be all alone" preceded his sick, sorry chuckle.

Our game continued for months. Whenever Marilyn went too far, we'd have our most touching moments. I was Frank's lumination in his seasons of privation, his temporary light when the sun lost eminence in his sky. How did it feel to be his artificial source of light?

It was only when some folly in the world bore too striking a resemblance to our relationship that I rebelled. I'd see a movie or hear about someone else's antics from Carol, who could publish an encyclopedia on the subject, and see myself too acutely reflected. The minister down the block was found bare-assed in the choir loft with a homely blonde parishioner. The fourth-grade teacher in the Catholic school that Riley's children used to attend was discovered with a janitor in a rather dark closet. These pathetic humans, driven by passion to the end of the curve of the known world, could have been me. Except for luck and Frank's moderation, I might warrant a page in Carol's almanac.

I'm no different, I'd think, as Carol regaled me with her latest chapter of local hearts broken: Dave Drew, home from college, asked out Riley's fourteen-year-old daughter, who still sucks her thumb at night. Carol's lawyer friend Charlotte, a fellow at several conservative think tanks, fell in love with the Jiffy Lube manager and ran away with him to Guatemala. Due to our friendship, my own rendition was above the fray. Sometimes to test her, I'd interrupt a story with "How is this different from me and Frank?"

True, we were discreet. True, we met by chance, no ads placed, no goods exchanged beyond our solemn words.

"You're different because you're you and Frank's Frank," or "You're so much subtler, dear," she'd say. "Most of these lovesick folks are as obvious as Hue." Hue, the grocery clerk from hell, was our touchstone. She hated her new American life so profoundly that she'd shout at you in an unknown tongue if your products' bar codes weren't lined up with her scanner's electronic eye. Carol reminded me of Hue to get me off the hook.

On the hook now, a tale out of a book more sober than Carol's, I lie on my couch and give Guy a taste of what it's like to be human. First, I serenade him, but singing must approximate animal pain since his reaction to it is identical: embarrassment that he has witnessed his owner in such an indelicate situation, worry that he caused it, signaled by whining and a determined refusal to meet my eye.

To take the pressure off of him, I decide to turn on some television, but because it's two A.M., my choices are limited to televangelists, reruns of *Baywatch,* MTV, and all-night news. When I turn the dial again, it's a home shopping show hawking diamonds for $19.95. Diamonds? Don't words hold meaning anymore, I ask the unabashed screen. Why can't I just go to sleep?

Because in six hours—and here's where time comes in handy—visiting hours begin. I want to be there first thing in the morning. Because as soon as he wakes up, Danny will be twelve, and I want to hug him. I want to sequester myself in the memory of his birth and the eleven years of relative peace that followed. "How did you know to have me on my birthday?" my clever boy, aged four, once asked his grinning mother, who mussed his hair and gulped in his fearless laugh.

Fearlessness comes of innocence. Now there are dejected monosyllables and pleas to be forgotten: "Don't buy me anything," Danny told me on the phone. But I went to the bookstore and found him a few things: a book of Escher drawings and colored pencils, an atlas of the world, and a leather-bound copy of *To Kill a Mockingbird*: peace, hope, and justice all in red, shiny wrapping for my son who no longer is guiltless, for my son who has done the most awful thing a person can do.

I turn off the television and wind the comforter around my legs. Blanket, I rechristen the useless thing.

Birthday

LAST NIGHT DANNY tried to kill himself. They did call me, a nurse named Considine is insisting, but I'm dubious. In fact, I'm beyond doubtful because I was home before two A.M., and Danny's attempt was around midnight. Attempt shouldn't be the word. At approximately eleven fifty-seven A.M., moments before his age was to change, Danny took a plastic knife to his wrist. Superficial wounds, she tells me, a web of scratches and a little blood, but damage enough to have him transferred to a new floor, where all goods, including my proposed gifts, are contraband. I hand them over to the nonchalant Miss Considine, so I can see my boy.

"Mom," he says, when I enter his bare cell of a room. He is wearing official suicide garb, a gray beltless jumpsuit with snaps instead of buttons, elastic slippers, and no socks.

Maybe what he did meant nothing and should warrant no response. But I remember the pages of warnings to parents about the secret code of those wishing to die: Danny wanted nothing for his birthday; suicides want to give everything away. "Danny, why did you?" I ask in a pinched voice meant to be interpreted as composure.

"I don't know." He shrugs his diffident shoulders.

"Who's supposed to know?"

55

Danny massages his wrist, which is covered by a small fabric bandage, the kind you'd use on a torn cuticle or shoe blister.

"Excuse me," I tell my reticent son. "I'll be right back, honey." I go to seek the nurse, who hovers outside the glass-enclosed chamber.

"What was Danny doing last night when this started?" I ask Miss Considine.

"I don't know, ma'am," she says.

"Who *does* know?" my buzz-saw voice insists.

"The resident, Dr. Clark. I'll call him if you'd like."

"Please." I say, relieved she's caught my drift after only a sentence of shrieking. I sit in a waiting area meant to soothe its occupant: honey-colored carpet, small cinnamon flowers on the otherwise blank walls, one photo of an Ansel Adams winter scene, frozen waterfall, opposite the window that, due to its height, looks out on air. Why is the suicide floor the highest one in this building?

Tall and bearded, Dr. Clark is approaching and extending his woolly hand. I notice our healthy veins in the exchange, our virgin wrists.

"I hear you were on duty last night," I say, dispensing with introductions. "Why wasn't I called?"

"You were called, Mrs. Horvath."

"I was home by one-thirty. I wish you had tried a few more times."

"We did notify someone."

"Who was that someone?"

"Mr. Horvath."

"Mr. Horvath does not have custody of his son. I do."

"In any case, it wasn't a serious attempt. I wouldn't be overly distressed by it."

"Then why did you call anyone? Why did you call Mr. Horvath? Why can't Danny receive his birthday presents?"

"It's procedure. Tomorrow when the regular staff is in, there'll be an evaluation. If they agree with my report, which emphasizes the lack of sincerity of his attempt, Danny will be sent back to his regular quarters and be given back his things, including your gifts."

"Today is Danny's birthday. Would you guess the two events might have a connection?"

"Possibly."

"And would you also guess that a child in his circumstance would benefit from today being as normal as possible?"

"Yes."

"And would you also concede that getting presents on a birthday, having a cake, lighting candles, could improve his present state of mind?"

"Maybe."

"Then let me give him his presents, for heaven's sakes. Let me have lunch with him and put this little candle in whatever dessert we're given. Don't take his birthday away, please."

"I wish I could cooperate fully, but we're bound by procedure. He can't have the gifts, but you can eat lunch together and light the candle as long as there's supervision in the room."

"I'm his mother. Isn't he safe with me?"

"Mrs. Horvath, we're burdened with rules that don't make too much sense at times. This is one of them," Dr. Clark smiles meekly.

Back in the glass suite under the eyes of bored nurse Considine, who must hate to work Sundays, I've stuck a blue candle into Danny's wobbly Jell-O. I take the matches from my purse and wonder why I haven't been searched more completely, given their precautions. We watch the small fire sway as we breathe gravely in its direction. "Happy birthday," I whisper to keep the celebration private. "I'll get you your presents tomorrow if I have to sneak them in under my coat," I smile.

"I didn't want presents, Mom." Exasperation fuels his words.

"Danny, I know what you said. I know what happened and how you feel, but if you're ever going to get out of here, you're going to have to make a choice."

"What do you mean?" he asks with small inquisitive eyes.

"You're going to have to stop screwing around with knives, even little plastic ones, and show these people you can stand to live."

I'm crying and shaking like it's the tundra here, and Danny is trembling, too.

"C'mon," I say, "I have an idea." I lead with my body across the room. Miss Considine looks up. She must wonder about our destination in this twelve-foot square. Dumbly, Danny follows me to the sealed window, where we observe the dirty snow fringing the parking lot and beyond it, the naked trees and lake. When my Australian friends visited last winter, they couldn't believe that it was frozen in February. Today, the ice is melting in tweedy patches about a hundred feet from shore.

"See? It's almost spring out there, Danny. I want you out of here and back in that world soon."

"Don't you remember?"

"Remember what?"

"Eddie."

"I know, honey."

"Well?"

"I believe you, that it was a mistake. Do you believe that?"

"I think that, but . . . ," and then he's silent.

"But what?"

". . . if it wasn't an accident?" his thin voice questions.

"What do you mean?"

"I mean, don't people know what they're doing?"

"Not all the time. . . . Sometimes."

"Did I know what I was doing?"

"I can't say. Did you want to hurt Eddie?" I whisper gravely.

"No way."

"Then what do you mean?"

"I knew how to work the bow. How could Eddie get killed?"

"People don't always think straight. Like last night. You didn't really want to kill yourself, did you?"

"No," he answers tearily.

"And when you shot that thing, when that arrow came out, you didn't really mean to hit Eddie . . ."

"It just came out and Eddie was dead."

We slump to the floor and weep onto each other's necks. Miss Considine doesn't acknowledge our whimpering duet. She's come to excel at discretion, which merely means looking away.

Rita and the Wolf

"WHEN I WAS nine, there was a new girl in class. Rita was a slip of a thing with a big nose and greasy brown hair. People asked her why her hair never looked clean, and Rita explained that she put mayonnaise in it to make it shine. When we laughed at her explanation, she said her mother was from Rumania, and that's what she had done as a girl there.

"Every bit of information armed us against her. We were like bees, attracted to the nectar of her strangeness. If her hair wasn't enough to single her out, she also lisped. 'Rita, thay thoup,' we teased in the lunch line.

"Early in the year, it became our sport to bait Rita constantly. If there was a puddle, Rita's new loafers would get baptized in it. If there was snow, Rita would christen its arrival with her unwilling outline. When we had a substitute and crazy Pat Maginnes couldn't behave, she'd say she was Rita. Rita's name would go up on the board in guilty letters for Miss Larkin to see on her return. If Rita protested, we'd tell Miss Larkin that Rita was lying, that she acted up behind Miss Larkin's back.

"Although we never spoke the rules of Rita's inquisition, they were clear to everyone. 'Rita pushed me,' one girl claimed. 'Rita thays bad words,' Lanny Bordeaux shouted.

"And Rita never protested. She had given up from the start, as if it wasn't worth the trouble to defend herself.

"That winter there was going to be a class play. Miss Larkin said we should write down our ideas and that the best idea would win. I wrote a script about inventions, which we were studying at the time. It was a radio show in which famous inventors were interviewed. When Rita asked me what I was doing, I told her I'd written a play about a girl raised by wolves. I said I hoped that Rita could star in it.

"Rita had no play idea herself, so all that week, she acted real friendly to me. Her face glowed with my attention as I spun more and more elaborate plans involving Rita in my fake production.

"'First you'll have to dress like a real little girl,' I said. "Come dressed like that tomorrow, and we'll practice at my house after school. But right now, howl like a wolf.

"'Why?' Rita asked.

"'That's how the girl talks. Now try it.'

"'Right here?' Rita asked, embarrassed.

"'Do it!' I baited her.

"'Okay,' she said. Then she opened her mouth and let out a blood-curdling howl. All the kids on the playground stopped in their tracks.

"Meanwhile, I had run away and was watching from near the swings. When Rita realized she'd been tricked, she burst into tears. It was the only time I saw her cry.

"All that week Rita refused to meet my eye. By Friday I was thinking that I was sorry, but I never told Rita."

"Kids are like that," Carol assures me.

She's smiling at the cruel tale I've just told her over coffee and an old donut in my kitchen. If I could forget about Danny, it would seem like a normal evening at home. I could pretend that Danny's in the front room playing a video game with the sound turned down in deference to Carol and me. Carol adds more fake cream to her coffee and offers consolation in psychology.

"They're afraid of things, Nancy, so they find someone more afraid. What happened to Rita anyway?"

"Her father died, and they moved away." My own story has depressed me and led me back to my only theme. "Was Danny afraid?"

"Was Danny ever afraid?" she mocks. "Isn't everyone? Remember when Nan stuttered? When she slouched like a noodle? When she would answer by nodding her head? When her scowl was permanent? Every kid is afraid. Well, so what?"

"So everything. I keep thinking about Rita. My parents were angry people. They made me nervous. I took it out on Rita for no good reason at all." I wish I smoked. I'd have a cigarette now. I am left to hair tugging and hand wringing, which I'm turning into an art form.

"And Danny had a good reason? Is that your point?"

"I don't know, Carol. I just think about it. Who wouldn't?"

"Well, I wouldn't worry, Nancy. Danny liked Eddie, and he was happy that you and Frank . . ."

"Me and Frank what?"

"He was happy that Frank was so fond of you."

"Danny knew about me and Frank?" I hear my breath wheezing. We are back in the ampitheater of my fears. "No."

"He told me you were seeing Frank, Nancy. I assumed you knew."

"What did he say . . . exactly?"

"He said that Eddie's mom didn't like Frank and that she didn't care if you were his friend."

"And who told him that?"

"Eddie, I'd guess. Or Marilyn, from what I know of her. She was pretty outspoken, wasn't she? I thought nothing of it at the time."

"Should I tell Schulien?"

"I'd tell him anything that might help Danny."

"Will this help Danny, Carol?"

"I can't see how," she says, offering me a commiserating little scowl over her coffee cup.

The Story

WHAT IS THE story and what isn't? A boy shoots another boy. One boy dies. That could be the story if there were no reason for more. Or, simpler still. A boy is dead. Another isn't. Even more clean, more factual. But facts have a way of tripping over themselves on their way to being understood. Why did the boy shoot? Was there something the boy knew that was troubling him? Did he aim at more than his target? What did he kill?

Two answers to everything, a plot that can be read like one of those comics that tells one story as you read it front to back, another when you turn it upside down and read it back to front.

A child accidentally shoots another. It is terrible. It causes great suffering. All feel the loss.

Or, a child wanting revenge for the unfairness of circumstance lashes out. The object of his anger is related to the cause of his pain. He is fatherless. The other child has a father. He wants that father.

And his mother has that father for herself.

He knows what grown-ups do. He's seen his mother leave late at night in a car without headlights. He's seen her pretend distance between herself and the man who touches her breasts. He's heard her furtive calls late at night after she's supervised his bedtime hygiene and tucked him in. What does she think she's doing sneaking around like a spy? Who is she fooling?

In one maneuver he can end all this by causing more pain. He can hurt people more than he's ever been hurt. He can have power beyond all the liars and hypocrites who say they love him. Really one liar, one hypocrite.

Mom, I shot Eddie.

What?

Look in the front room.

What are you saying?

Just look.

Before her, incontrovertible, the evidence. The boy has told the truth. The body is too pale to hope for a lie.

If only I hadn't known the man, the mother thinks. If only I had been perfectly pure.

If it were just a story, the mother thinks. If it were just a story.

Talk Show

"TURN ON CHANNEL thirty-two," Carol says, "and call me later."

I tune in during a commercial for toilet tissue. Some products are so basic, what's the point of advertising, but, oh well. Then Kathy Lee sings about a cruise to the Caribbean. I'd love to take me and Danny on a cruise to most anywhere. Once my dad took us to Hawaii for Christmas. Just smelling the air was a gift.

After the theme song, the guests are reintroduced, and before words become necessary, I see Marilyn. The subject is mothers who have lost their children to violence, and Carol has cued me in to her quarter of an hour.

Marilyn looks good. She's tipped her hair again and is wearing a little black dress with a red scarf. She's listening with wide eyes as Jerry Spitzer re-creates Eddie's death.

"And then your husband got a call from next door, is that correct?"

"Yes," she barely speaks.

"And who was that, Marilyn?"

"It was my neighbor, the boy's mother."

"And what did she say?"

"She told him to come over fast, that something had happened."

"And when he got there . . ."

"They had already gone to the hospital."

"And when you finally arrived at the hospital, what did you see?"

"They told me my son was gone."

"And as I shared with the audience before, this was a shooting accident?"

"Right."

"How was it that they were playing with a gun?"

"It was a hunting bow. My husband hunts and he took the children. Eddie . . . my son . . . brought it next door and then. . . ."

Marilyn is wailing and Jerry Spitzer is patting her back. They pan the audience and I see the mothers of Chicago sharing her grief.

"Now, I know this is hard, Mrs. Nova, but can you go on?"

"They were playing a game," she sobs.

"And what did the arrow do?"

"It hit him in the chest. He died immediately."

"And what has it done to your family?"

"My husband and I are separated. My daughter and I are in therapy. I never imagined something like this. . . ."

Now the theme song is playing and it's time for another commercial. But before that I hear that we'll return to her story, which involves another surprise.

Marilyn's dried her eyes and is back on the screen. The way the emotion has been drained from her face makes her appear calm. She looks like she's on automatic now.

"So tell me, Marilyn, what did you find out about your husband after this terrible accident?"

"I found out he'd been seeing the next-door neighbor."

"You mean the mother of the boy . . ."

"Yes."

"And what did you think when you heard this?"

"What anyone would think, that I've lost everything to this woman."

"So?" Carol is asking me cautiously. She's shown up in person, three minutes after everyone watching television has received the news.

"I think the whole world knows."

"Let's have some coffee," Carol says, busy with beans and filters in the kitchen to avoid my eyes.

"Why, Carol?"

"Why what?" she replies, coffee beans whining their way to grounds.

"Why did she go on the show?"

"She wants the world to know what happened," she smiles meekly.

"Nothing she said wasn't true," I say, voice clenched until it breaks. And now the phone is ringing and I fear the worst: my mother has seen the show. I will have to tell her what it was Marilyn meant, which, of course, explains itself so well. "Now mother . . ." I hear myself begin when a different voice interrupts.

"Nancy, we need to talk," Frank is saying. "Can you meet me tonight when I get off of work?"

"I guess so," I say blankly. "Where?"

"Come by the station. We can take my car and go somewhere."

"Midnight?"

"Right."

"Did you hear her . . . Marilyn . . . on TV?"

"Yes."

"Did you know . . . I mean did she tell you she was doing the show?"

"You know Marilyn. What does she tell me?"

"So . . ."

"Pull up behind the station. Park your car and wait for me."

"Okay," I pause, pulse clanking in my ears. "You're sure you want to talk to me?"

"Yes."

"Okay."

As simple as that, it's over.

"Who were you whispering to?"

"Joyce, from work," I explain.

There's something about Frank that goes hand in hand with subterfuge. I should tell Carol, who knows everything about me: my bra size, 34A; how my left eye gets puffier than my right when I cry; how, when Danny was born, I got carried away with enthusiasm and temporarily quit my job; how Carol's sister Jerrie helped me get it back. I should tell her about Frank—but I don't.

Around Midnight

I BUNDLE MYSELF into a black fleece-lined coat and some old leather boots. My hair is too long, but I haven't had time to be vain—to cut my hair or shop for some lipstick or think much at all about how I look anymore. I must be a sight, I think, when I see a woman wearing a wool and gabardine jacket with matching slacks. She has on those new shoes that look like Edwardian boots. And her hair is freshly cut, and her nails are manicured so the moons of her fingernails are as even as tombstones. Everything's in place for her. She doesn't even know that Danny and I exist.

That's the fundamental difference between me and the rest of the world, their ignorance, my knowledge. But don't think I'm the only one who's ever felt so dislocated from my life. Think about a woman in Sarajevo out to buy a loaf of bread when a bomb goes off near her home and kills her whole family. Think about a mother not far from here wondering if her son will ever make it home tonight because he's not a gang member and has to walk through enemy territory.

How's that different from Danny and me?

Danny's the shooter. Danny's the one who launched the bomb. Danny's the one who's made the neighborhood unsafe.

The Station

MIDNIGHT COMES AND goes and suddenly (I must have been asleep), I feel a hand on my head and Frank's late-night husky voice whispering, "Let's go inside. The first floor is empty." Rubbing my eyes and looking at Frank's face, I notice two new features, a small beard that must have grown since Eddie died, and a look in his big, watery eyes that reminds me of my own grief.

I hurry after him, thinking it odd that I'm not walking beside him. In the past when we'd met at night, there were long welcoming ceremonies right in public. We would kiss each other's mouths as if we were tasting a rare confection. Now, watching his back and calves and heels in front of me, what does Frank resemble? A stranger in a hurry. Is there a fire or something, I ask myself. My mind sometimes punishes me with its levity. Who says our emotions can lead our intellect anywhere?

In all the months that I've known Frank, I've never been inside the firehouse or even wondered how it looked. Once inside, it seems familiar because it's the standard Chicago field house and recreation design. Some friend of the mayor must have the cinder block concession, another a corner on the offensive green paint of Chicago walls from City Hall to

O'Hare Airport. Fluorescent lights are everywhere and a tomblike silence, as if we have entered a deserted barracks somewhere in space.

Frank, however, is not waiting. He is about a hallway ahead of me on his march to somewhere. From this distance he could be any man rather than the one whose calves strained and ached because he liked me to kneel at the edge of the mattress as he entered me from behind. I loved that about Frank, his desire to penetrate me as deeply as he could, as if in doing so, he could know me more intimately. Some women complain that it isn't the most practical position for them. For us it was a measure of trust. It said that when we faced each other, we understood so much that we could stand to turn away. Back to chest, buttocks to pelvis was an economy fully endowed by our affection.

My mind never wandered then, but now I can't stop wondering. Is he afraid to look me in the eyes? How do lovers change their language? Even if their tongues and nipples and stomachs discover a way to reconcile, their lips don't form words.

Frank rounds a corner, and I follow him into what looks like a daycare nursery. There are three knee-high cots, some pillows strewn in a corner, several folded gray blankets, and a few baskets on wheels that could serve as makeshift dressers. There are only overhead lights, so options are limited. Frank chooses no light at all, so I fumble in the dark squinting in his direction.

Frank motions from the farthest corner of the room. "Come here," he says softly. I can identify in his voice the static that fills mine whenever I think about our doom.

I glide in his direction but stop short because I feel like falling onto his chest and sobbing, but I'm certain that our new rules forbid such comfort. As soon as I pause, perhaps two feet away, Frank lunges and grips me. He squeezes my shoulders and chest against him until they are concave. His body is a knot that I have tied for eternity.

"Frank," I say desperately, but nothing sensible can follow. "I shouldn't be here," I breathe into his neck.

Even as Frank wrenches me closer and closer, tight-fisted hands grabbing my shoulders, I know that he can't hold me. His mind is with Eddie. I knew this before I even saw him.

"What is this room for?" I ask to break his wrestler's grasp. Like a sleepy butler, he steps back and offers his bent elbow for me to lay my coat on. I oblige. My dress follows. I seat myself knees up on this low cot, wearing just my patterned black tights, and my lifeless white bra and my boots, and Frank moves toward me. He hasn't taken off one article of clothing. He hasn't said my name, which used to hang in the air like perfume when we made love. Am I who I used to be?

He presses me back on the bed, and without a word, digs his body into mine as if our weights could tunnel us into the floor and erase our existence. We lie atop the tortured cot, rocking up and down, Frank fully clothed, me almost naked. Soon, I feel him unzipping his pants and arching up his back so he can pull down my tights and stick his penis in. I've become very wet, but he isn't fully erect. When I try to touch him there, he pushes my hand away. "No," he says in a voice flat as sand. He massages his penis and gets it inside me. I lie completely still, afraid to move, afraid to speak. And as he rocks on top of me and groans, all I want to say is, "I'm sorry, Frank," a simple phrase that means that Eddie is dead, that our lives are ruined, that we can't be lovers, that my son is locked away, that Frank can't look at me, that I can't touch him, that we can't make love.

By the time that I finish my litany of regrets, Frank's body is huge and strange and silent, and my breasts feel cold. Only his breath on the pillow indicates that we're alive. "Frank," I say and nothing else.

"Frank," I continue. "I'm so sorry."

"You don't know," Frank whispers.

"I . . ." I begin to say I do, but Frank is seized by sobbing. "I pity you," I want to tell him, but in pity, there's no room for love.

When I caress his hair, Frank nearly flinches and is off me. He turns away and tucks himself in and hands me my things, piece by awkward piece. I begin dressing as Frank flees the room. And after I have put on my coat, I walk to the front door, where he is waiting with a ring of keys.

As he opens the door, I hear him say something that sounds like sorry but might just be sorrow. Maybe he's saying that sorrow is much deeper than what we ever had.

I look back into the building, but by the time I've turned around, he's disappeared.

Part Two

His Story

"EDDIE PRETENDED HE was shooting me. Then I pretended I was shooting him."

"What time was it?"

"It was about four forty-five because Eddie got home from his school around four o'clock, and then we walked the dog."

"What kind of school did Eddie go to?"

"Catholic school."

"Did you see Eddie often after school?"

"Usually a few days a week."

"Did you play with him on weekends?"

"We played all the time."

"And what kind of games did you and Eddie play after school?"

"Sometimes video games. Sometimes pretend games."

"And on this day, who decided what game to play?"

"I guess we both did."

"Did you both usually decide?"

"I'd let Eddie decide a lot because he was younger."

"What was the age difference, Daniel?"

"A year."

"And you're how old?"

"Almost twelve."

"And on the day we're discussing, how did the compound bow get in the house?"

"Eddie brought it over."

"It was Eddie's bow?"

"Yes."

"And how did it happen that you shot him?"

"I was pretending to fire it at him like he had a few times before at me. It just shot out and hit him."

"Did Eddie hold it first?"

"Yes."

"And did it ever 'just shoot out' when Eddie held it?"

"No."

"But it just 'shot out' like that for you."

"Yes."

"Had you used a compound bow before?"

"Yes, when Frank, Mr. Nova, took us hunting."

"When was the last time before the day in question that you had used it?"

"I never used this one. This one was Eddie's new one, but in December we went deer hunting."

"And did you shoot a deer?"

"Frank did."

"And who taught you how to release the compound bow?"

"Mr. Nova showed us."

"And did you have safety training in bow hunting?"

"Mr. Nova took us to two days of training."

"And why did he do that?"

"Because kids are required to get trained if they're going to hunt with bows in Wisconsin."

"And what were some things you were taught in the safety class?"

"We were taught never to aim bows at people."

"And Eddie took the same course?"

"Yes."

"But he aimed the bow at you, and you aimed it at him?"

"Yes."

"Daniel, can you illustrate on this picture of a compound bow how you release it?"

"Yes."

"Can you say it in words?"

"Not really. Well, maybe I can. You're holding your bow in your left hand. You take your arrow and notch it, pull back on the draw string and release it when you're ready."

"Did the safety course tell you never to fire a bow in the house?"

"Yes."

"And never at close range?"

"Yes."

"So after the bow was fired at Eddie Nova in your house, in the front room, wasn't it?"

"Yes . . ."

"Why didn't you get help, Daniel?"

"Eddie was dead."

"How did you know he was dead?"

"I've seen dead people on TV, and Eddie wasn't breathing."

"Did he die immediately?"

"I think so."

"You shot him and he died without . . ."

"There was blood under him all over the place and for a few seconds . . ."

"And for a few seconds . . . ?"

"Eddie looked at me."

"If he looked at you, wasn't he alive?"

"For a few seconds."

"And then?"

"And then he was just staring."

"And what does that mean?"

"It means you're dead."

"How do you know that?"

"When Mr. Nova shot the deer, it was just staring."

"Before Eddie began staring, did you try to help him?"

"I held him and put him on the floor. I shouted his name. He looked at me."

"Even if you assumed he was dead, wouldn't it have been wise to get help anyway?"

"Sure."

"Then why didn't you?"

"I was so scared I wasn't thinking right."

"If you had been thinking right, what would you have done?"

"I would have called 911 and gotten his mom or dad. His dad's a paramedic."

"But you didn't do that."

"No."

"What did you do instead?"

"I hid under the porch."

"How long did you hide for?"

"A half hour or so. Until my mom came home."

"Daniel, were you alone after school the days your mother was at work?"

"Yes."

"For how long were you alone?"

"For usually an hour."

"Did you ever speak to your mother at work?"

"I called her as soon as I got home every day."

"And were there rules for being home alone?"

"Yes."

"Were you allowed to have guests?"

"Not really, but Eddie . . ."

"Yes?"

". . . was allowed over."

"Wasn't he a guest?"

"We were always together, so I thought my mom would think it was okay for me to have him."

"Did your mother know you played with Eddie when she wasn't around?"

"Yes, I think."

"What does that mean, Daniel?"

"I mean I told her Eddie had been over, or she saw me in our yard or in front of his house, and she never said anything."

"On this particular day, you stated that Eddie brought over the compound bow. Had he ever done that before, Daniel?"

"Not really."

"What do you mean, 'not really'?"

"He once called and asked if he should, and I said no."

"Why did you say no?"

"Because it was dangerous."

"So you knew it was dangerous."

"Yes."

"Then why didn't you say no when Eddie asked you this time?"

"He didn't ask."

"What do you mean, Daniel?"

"He just showed up with it."

"And then what happened?"

"I let him in, and we watched some TV. We walked Guy—

that's my dog. Then we came back in, and he started fooling around with it. He aimed it at Guy, and I told him not to do that. Then he aimed it at me."

"Did you think Eddie would shoot you or Guy?"

"Not really."

"Did you worry a little about that?"

"I guess so."

"Had Eddie ever hurt you or your dog?"

"Once he took our dog for a whole day and kept it."

"Did he ask permission?"

"No, the dog got out of the yard, and he just brought it to his house and didn't tell us."

"And you spent the day looking for the dog and worrying?"

"Yes."

"On this particular day, how long did you play with the compound bow?"

"For maybe twenty minutes or so."

"And were you angry at Eddie, Daniel?"

"No."

"Were you a little angry that he aimed the bow at you and the dog?"

"Maybe a little."

"Did you and Eddie ever quarrel?"

"Yes, but mainly it was no big deal."

"What would a typical quarrel be? Can you recall one?"

"Once we were fishing and Eddie was spoiling the fun."

"Can you give an example?"

"Instead of being quiet, he was running around and throwing rocks in the water, and then he tossed my cap in the river."

"And then what happened?"

"Mr. Nova had to try to get it out of the river."

"No, I mean what happened between you and Eddie?"

"I told Eddie I felt sorry for his father."

"Why?"

"Because Eddie could never behave."

"And what did Eddie do?"

"He punched me and called me a bad name."

"What name did he call you?"

"He called me faggot."

"Danny, would you say you were good with the compound bow?"

"I was just learning."

"Is it easy or hard to fire a compound bow?"

"The one Eddie had is pretty easy to fire because it's made for a kid. It has twenty pounds of pull. I'd have trouble with an adult's bow because there's more pull."

"But this was a children's bow."

"Yes. But it's not like it's so simple. You still have to know the steps."

"So you had to know what you were doing to make it just 'shoot out.'"

"Right. But I guess Eddie had engaged it when he was pointing it at me."

"You'd still say it was an accident?"

"Because I didn't mean to shoot."

"Were you excited to be using it?"

"Not really."

"Were you having fun up until that point?"

"Not really. I thought of asking Eddie to leave and I didn't."

"I bet you wish that day never happened."

"All the time."

"What do you imagine when you think of the day never happening?"

"If Mom had left her work a little early, if I had basketball practice on Wednesdays instead of Tuesdays, if Mrs. Nova told Eddie to watch Carly. If Mr. Nova didn't hunt. If my mother hadn't made me go hunting with Mr. Nova."

"You didn't want to go hunting?"

"Not really."

"Why do you suppose your mom made you?"

"She must have thought some things were good for boys to do. Like hunting."

"And how do you feel when you think about the day?"

"Very sad and very sorry."

"I was wondering, Danny, who are you sorry for?"

"For Eddie and my mom and the Novas."

"Are you sorry for yourself?"

"I guess so."

"And why are you sorry for yourself?"

"Because this should have never happened."

"If you hadn't shot the bow, Eddie would still be alive. Right?"

"Right."

"Do you have any questions, Danny?"

"Not really."

"Are you sure?"

"Well, just one. Can I stop talking now?"

Wrist

I'VE NEVER REALLY known a crazy person, so when they ask me if I think I'm crazy, it's hard to know what to say. People look at me like they think I'm crazy, but I don't think they mean to, and I'm not sure if their look means I'm crazy or they're just worried that I am.

My mom is so careful with me. She doesn't want to get mad or raise her voice about this. God, when I left a sweatshirt on the floor or ate corn chips in my room and didn't clean up the crumbs, she was angrier than she is about Eddie. She must be real angry at me, but maybe she's afraid to show it for just that reason. She thinks I'm crazy and doesn't know what to do.

I know how she feels. Sometimes I'd see a homeless man on Broadway when I walked to school. He wore rags around his feet and a skirt made of garbage bags instead of pants. He talked to himself all the time. I was sure he was crazy, so when he'd say things to me, even normal things, like, "Hi, young man, going to school?" I'd look away. I started walking a different way to avoid him. All spring I did that until near the end of school, I went my regular old way, and he was gone. Then I wondered what had happened to him. I worried that somehow my walking a different way had affected him. I mean, maybe he used to be a father and talking to me was like talking to his own kid. Maybe when I went the other way, he couldn't take it anymore. But I went the other way because I was afraid. I didn't really think what talking to me might have meant to him until much later.

Anything is possible, I keep thinking. That's another way I'm different since Eddie died. Sometimes Eddie would say crazy things. He had a good imagination. Once he said, "Let's run away, Danny. I know where my dad keeps money."

"No way," I answered. "Even if we had somewhere to go, our parents would find us in about three minutes. Your dad and my mom are real smart. They wouldn't just let us disappear."

"I guess not," Eddie said like he was embarrassed.

Now though, I think about it. If Eddie and I had run away, we would have been found. Then maybe my mom and his dad would have said we couldn't be together anymore. If Eddie couldn't see me, he couldn't have brought the bow to our house. If Eddie couldn't have brought the bow, I couldn't have shot it.

I keep thinking about all these *ifs*. Then I think about what really happened. And I always see it as a picture of what did happen. I don't see myself shooting. I see Eddie lying on the floor. I see his body there. Sometimes at night that's all I can see in my room when I close my eyes. The room is gone, the window is gone, there's just me and Eddie. And everything is still, like someone has painted a picture of me with Eddie's body. Eddie's body looks bigger, but my eyes are seeing it like it happened a minute ago.

Does it mean I'm crazy that I feel so bad? Does it mean I'm crazy that maybe I'll never feel better?

That's what I was thinking when I started sawing on my wrist. I knew I couldn't really do much, just like Eddie knew we couldn't really run away and get away with it. But it was fun to try.

Each day when I wake up, I have this strange experience. I open my eyes, and it seems like the old days before this all happened. I stretch and start feeling good because it's a new day. The sun comes in the room and lands on my face, and I play games with it by closing one eye and then the other.

But then I remember. Sometimes the truth comes back in a flash. Other times I get a sick feeling in my chest and I feel afraid before I know why.

There's just a few seconds of peace before it all comes back to me: the day, the hour, the moment that changed my life forever. It's all scooped out of time like a short movie, maybe a rock video, only there's no music. There are no words or sounds at all. It's a silent movie until my mother finds me under the porch. Her lips are moving, but I don't hear any sound. We go into the house and see Eddie lying on the floor. My mother listens to his chest. She grabs his wrist. She feels his neck. And then she holds his body and the sound begins. She says in a quiet, cool voice, "Get me the phone." I bring her the portable phone and she calls 911. And she calls Frank at work and gets him on the line. Then she holds me and Eddie both until the police show up and the ambulance.

What's funny is that I can't see myself. I see my mother and I see Eddie. Instead of her holding on to me, I see her holding on to Eddie like he's the living one and I'm the dead one.

And in a sense it's true. Eddie's dead and I'm dead, too. I killed us both.

· · ·

The doctors say it will help me to write down everything that I remember about Eddie and me. They say I should start when we first met. Every day I promise that I'll start, but I never get beyond this memory. Maybe tomorrow I'll begin the story. If I can find the words.

The Boy Next Door

by Danny Horvath

I MET EDDIE when I was ten and a half and Eddie was nine and a half. That's when we moved onto Elmdale. I remember a few things about the day we moved. First I remember how bright the sky looked. It was late fall and the light is usually kind of dull—like the year has worn it out. But the sky was very blue, blue as a robin's egg, my mom said, and that's a good sign. My mom is Nancy. She's a short pretty lady with light brown hair and a big smile. She's been divorced since I was two. I don't even remember when we lived with my dad, Alex. And I really haven't seen him that much until this all happened. He has a new family, and my mom says that he's happy now. Because his new family makes him so happy, he doesn't see too much of his old one.

Mom was so glad that we'd be living in our own house instead of an apartment. Not that our apartment was so crummy, but she said that anything you don't own is crummy—period. So we got this big old house on Elmdale that looked kind of haunted because the old people who lived in it hadn't kept it up too well. The outside of the house had those ugly shingles that look like unmatched socks stuck all over it, and the stairs were rotten in some places. Inside it smelled like a lot of food had been burned there. But my mom is real smart about making things better if she can. She came into the house and before she even unpacked one box, she made bread. That made things smell good.

We were standing around and waiting for Aunt Sheila to maybe come and visit when the doorbell rang. My mom thought it also might be Carol, who lives close by, and my mom knows from work. My mom says that Carol is a "cool customer." She says that Aunt Sheila is a "wacky lady." When she opened the door, she said, "Danny, I think it's for you, honey."

When I looked through the screen I saw a kid who was shorter than me but maybe my age. He had on a Bears sweatshirt and no coat so either no one had seen him leave the house or he didn't even know it was cold out. That's what my mom says about me, that I don't even know when I'm cold. The kid had a loud voice. He announced that he was Eddie and that he lived next door.

I just stood there looking at him. But then my mom laughed and said, "Danny, don't you want to ask him in?" and I said "Yeah, sure," or something and opened the door. And Mom told him I was Danny and she was Nancy. I don't know if Eddie heard that because as soon as Mom opened the door, he just came bounding in. My mom said he reminded her of a big friendly dog the way he settled down in our front room before there was hardly anything in it that first day. Soon he said he wanted to see my room, but my room was like a cave with nothing in it. "All right," I said, and showed him my room, which is all by itself on the first floor behind the kitchen. My mom thought I'd have more privacy that way. When I got older, I'd be really thankful for privacy, she said.

So Eddie and I are standing in my empty room, which isn't that big. Eddie seems to like it so much that he's cruising all around it and rubbing his hand on the wall like he's petting it.

It's cold outside, but when Eddie gets to the window that looks out on his house next door, he tries to open it. I know he lives there because Carol told us that some kids lived in the house on our left.

At first the window won't budge. Paint has sealed over the opening, but then Eddie uses his hand to hammer at it, and suddenly the window comes loose and Eddie pulls it all the way up. "From now on I'll come over this way. It's closer," he smiles.

And I nod okay but I hope he's just kidding 'cause I don't think my mom will want people barging in the windows instead of using the doors now that she finally has her own house. "We have to treat this place like it's special," she's already told me, "because it is special. It's our very own place."

"What should be our password?" Eddie asks.

"What do you mean?"

"Well, you won't always be in your room. So maybe I can pound three times and when you hear me you can come to the window. Let's try it now."

"Okay," I say but when I just stand there instead of leaving the room so Eddie can crawl out and try it, he shakes his head.

I'm new to all this. None of my friends lived on my block before when we had the apartment, so I'm not that used to playing with kids in my house, especially before we make plans. I'm not even used to having a house. So Eddie finally says, "Leave the room, will you?" I walk into the kitchen, where my mom is standing. She's pretending to ignore me so I can have my privacy with my new friend.

All of a sudden I hear three hard knocks, long and slow and strong like Eddie's hand is bigger than a kid's hand. I walk into my room and wave at him through the window, and I raise it to let him in.

After Eddie comes in we talk about how well that worked. Then Eddie asks me if I have toys, and my mom, even though she's pretending she's not listening, drags in my two big boxes of things that aren't clothes and starts setting up my room for me. "Put your toys anywhere for now," she says. But she's already carried in this red metal shelf she got at resale that's supposed to be for my toys and my books, so Eddie and me start unpacking. Before you know it, it's suppertime, and Eddie and me have been together all day.

"Does Eddie want to stay for supper?" my mom asks. She's leaning against my door and admiring the way I set up all my toys though Eddie by now has taken down about half my things to play with and to look at.

"That's okay," Eddie says. "My mom wants me home because there's a sitter coming, and she needs to know where I am."

"Hasn't she known where you are all day?" my mom asks.

"I don't know," Eddie smiles. "Well, I'd better go," he says, and then right in front of my mom, whose eyes get wide while he does this, he opens the bedroom window, jumps out, closes it, and waves to me.

"See you tomorrow," he says with just his lips moving because the window is closed now. And me and my mom begin to laugh because the first day in our house has been a real surprise. And we're also laughing because before we moved I complained to my mom that we wouldn't know anyone on Elmdale or at my new school and now six hours haven't passed, and I have a new friend named Eddie.

2

FOR THE NEXT few days different people come and visit. Aunt Sheila brings red flowers in a blue vase which my mom puts on our new kitchen table. Our new kitchen table is really our old kitchen table with this shiny Mexican cloth on it. Sheila knows how much my mom likes blue. She's my grandmother's sister, but she's much nicer. My own grandma, I sometimes think, must be related to my father because she's never happy to see me or my mom. Maybe she needs a new family like he did. And Carol and Riley come to visit. I guess I've known Carol forever. She's older and bigger than my mom with red curls that always look messy. And Riley is this old guy she sees—he must be sixty, and he kind of looks like a pig, but I can tell that Carol really likes him. She's kind of old too, forty-five or so, and like I mentioned, kind of messy, so she really can't care too much how Riley looks. "I think Riley invented the turtleneck sweater," my mom once said, so now we call him Mr. Turtleneck but not to his face. They come around the time that Sheila does, and they bring over some Chinese food, which we're eating when I hear Eddie's fist pounding on my window.

"What's that?" Sheila asks, alarmed because she's the first to worry about most things. She hates big noises and won't even walk on the same side of the street as a man walking the other way. She thinks someone will grab her purse but so far, no one has.

"Just a ghost," I yell in her direction.

"Danny's new friend," my mom explains because she doesn't think it's nice to tease older ladies like Aunt Sheila. Aunt Sheila has never been married, and she really loves my mom and me. Sheila has green slanty eyes like a fox and very short gray hair. She's always looked like Peter Pan to me.

Eddie climbs right in the window and says, "What do I smell?"

"Chinese food," I explain.

"C'mon," Eddie says and heads right for the kitchen. Our only table seats four people, so after Eddie meets everyone and fills his plate, we settle down in the front room at my mom's cocktail table. It's a cool table because there's a built-in chess board, and I'm learning chess. Sometimes I play it with Riley, whose last name is, get this, Flowers. Riley Flowers. I think he lets me win but my mom doesn't. She's hard to beat at chess, and when I almost win I know I'm really getting good at the game.

"Do you play chess?" I ask Eddie. He's dangling a noodle like a worm from his hand and nearly crossing his eyes to look at it. He seems pretty distracted with his food and doesn't answer at first.

"I asked if you play chess."

"No way!" Eddie says.

"Some day I'll have to teach you."

"No way!" Eddie laughs and throws a chow mein noodle at me. I don't think my mom wants us throwing food in her new front room, so I say, "C'mon, Eddie. This house is brand new."

"It is not," he says. "It's old and smelly from the Millers."

Now I think that's pretty mean to say about our new place, so I just change the subject.

"How about checkers?" I ask.

"My dad and me play checkers a lot."

"Who is your dad?" I ask, but at the same time I'm thinking that Eddie's pretty rude. Maybe his dad needs to teach him a little better. I don't even have a dad, and I know how to act better than Eddie. Maybe it's because he's younger though. Maybe I acted this way, but I don't remember.

"My dad is Frank Nova. *Nova* means new. He's a fireman, and firemen play a lot of checkers."

"Do you ever go with him to fires?"

"No."

"Do you want to?"

"Maybe."

"So why don't you ask him?"

"I'm still hungry," Eddie says and takes off for the kitchen.

I see through to the other room that my mother is giving him a fresh plate with lots more noodles.

"Want some more?" she shouts to me.

"I'm full," I say, which makes me wonder why Eddie is so hungry. It's one o'clock on a Saturday, so he must have come over without lunch.

"Didn't your dad give you lunch?" I ask him.

"My dad's at work. It's my mom who didn't give me lunch."

"Who's your mom?"

"She's Marilyn, and she goes to the beauty shop on Saturdays. She takes Carly, who's my sister, but she doesn't take me because she says I can't stay still. That's why I can't eat chocolate or drink Coke either. Because I can't stay still," Eddie laughs and toasts me with his can of Coke.

I think Eddie would have stayed for dinner too that day, but I was supposed to be baby-sat by Aunt Sheila so my mom could go with Riley and Carol to an opera. When I listen to opera, it sounds pretty stupid to me with all those people shouting what's in the story, so I'm glad to be with Sheila. We'll watch old movies on TNT, drink hot chocolate that she buys at this Mexican grocery and mixes in a blender, and look at photos of my mom when she was younger. Sheila says my mom looks like Myrna Loy, but I don't really know who that is.

3

My GRANDMA LOVES cats, but she doesn't like people too
much. She likes to tell a story about how, when my mom was
little, she cried too much, and my grandma wanted to throw
her out the window but my grandpa stopped her. "I'm glad
Grandpa was nice!" I told my mom, and she laughed. But I bet
that story makes her real sad because it makes me feel pretty
lousy for her. Maybe they should have gotten divorced like my
mom and dad did if no one could be happy in that house.
Maybe Grandpa could have raised my mom before he got sick
and died.

When the doorbell rings, Grandma is smoking a cigarette
which she puts out by just throwing it on the wooden porch
and stomping on it before she comes into the house. She has
brought something in a bag which she hands to my mom. My
mom looks in the bag, and her eyes seem sort of puzzled. She
pulls out this old-looking cloth or something, and grandma
says, "Your old bedspread. From high school. Maybe you can
use it."

Now I'm thinking how I know she won't use that ugly thing
when I hear Eddie's knock on the window. Maybe he thinks we
have Chinese food again. Maybe he watches my house all the

time and comes over whenever he thinks we're going to eat something. I wonder who fed him before we got here.

"What's that noise?" my grandma shouts to me, and I'm seriously worried to tell her because not too many things are funny to her at all. Mom says she's sad that Grandpa was sick and died of cancer, but I bet she was sad even when Grandpa was well.

"It's my friend," I say quietly, but I mainly hope she's not listening anymore. Eddie is already in the window and the first thing he hears from Grandma is, "Hasn't your friend ever heard of doors?"

I'm worried that Eddie's feelings are going to be hurt, and my mom is too because she tells my grandma to come upstairs with her, but Eddie doesn't seem to mind. He's brought all these little red and blue and black bristly blocks that fit together, and he sits down right on my floor and starts to build a tower. By the end of the afternoon, Grandma goes home, and our tower almost reaches the ceiling.

After Grandma and Eddie go home, Mom breathes a sigh of relief and collapses into our old leather chair. "After Grandma visits," she says, "I always feel like we need to celebrate. If you weren't a kid, we'd share a beer!"

"I'll drink to that," I say. And we sit down the way we like, close to each other on our old couch, and we pull the comforter around us, and watch *America's Funniest Videos,* and pop microwave popcorn, and she falls asleep just when a dog is about to spray a man with a hose.

The next day was my first day of school, but Eddie attended Catholic school, so I guess I should skip school in this story. But I do remember that sometime during that first week of school, because Mom was just about to take me to get supplies, that Frank Nova came over and introduced himself. I think my mom thought he was kind of handsome because she smiled a lot when he visited. He looks like a TV guy from some hospital show, but I don't remember his name. On this first visit, Frank Nova tried to be real helpful. Mom had some heavy boxes she needed to store in our basement, and Frank carried them down there for her. Then they came upstairs and he asked her if she thought her furnace was working all right, and she said she didn't know. They went back into the basement together, and when they came up, she was talking about new filters and how she'd have to buy them this week. Frank promised to come over and help her change them. He also said that he was cooking his prize-winning chili right now and that he'd bring some over later. When my mom asked him about his wife, he didn't seem too eager to say much. "She's not a chili fan," Frank said quietly, "but you two should meet."

"Eddie's a great kid," my mom said.

"Well, everyone likes Eddie," but then I thought of my grandma and how what Frank said really isn't true, but I just was quiet about it.

Later that week my mom got the filters. She must have called Frank because he and Eddie came over through the door late that afternoon. My room was all set up now, so Eddie and me were able to play video games. My favorite is this one called Daytona, which is a driving game. I started playing as usual and showed Eddie how to do it, but it didn't go that well because Eddie couldn't wait for my turn to end. He grabbed the controls right out of my hand and started taking my turn, which wasn't very funny. I told him to stop and I called him a jerk, but he said, "No, I'm your guest," which he was. Still, it made me mad that Eddie was such a baby about things like this.

I was glad there was a kid next door, but sometimes, like now, I was kind of sad the kid was Eddie. It would have been more fun if someone like my friend Todd from my old school lived here instead. Some kids like Eddie might not think that Todd is very much fun because he's so little and has glasses, but he knows how to play any video game on Earth, and he's real good about sharing, and he'd never climb in a window instead of using a door. His dad is Chinese and his mom is Japanese, and neither of them knows English very well, but they're a nice family, and I used to like hanging around them. The Japanese have this day called Children's Day, where they'll take you anywhere you want to go and do anything you say. Once Todd took me along, and we went bowling and miniature golfing and to the Rock and Roll McDonald's all on the same day.

Soon I hear my mom and Frank back in the kitchen, and it looks like they're sitting down for coffee. I was hoping she'd start dinner, but I guess that'll happen later. Older people are more flexible about things like this than kids. I know when breakfast, lunch, and dinner happen, and I like that schedule to be followed. I guess since Frank doesn't live here, she doesn't want to serve him dinner. So it's five forty-five in the evening, but we're having cookies and coffee and milk. There's no telling when she'll get around to dinner.

It turns out that Frank likes ice skating, and he offers to take me and Eddie indoor skating on Saturday. It's his weekend off, he explains. "Maybe Marilyn and I can go, too!" my mom says, but Frank seems kind of slow in answering. He gives a look to Eddie, which maybe says, "I need to explain this, not you." And then he says that since Marilyn has the kids every week-end he works, she expects him to take the kids, Eddie and his little sister, Carly, on the weekends that he doesn't, which is fine with him, he says. But he seems a little aggravated about it or kind of embarrassed that Eddie's mom isn't that friendly. Maybe she's like my grandma, I start to think. Maybe they are another unhappy family, but I sure hope not. I hardly know any happy families, and since we're going to live here for a long time, it might be nice if they broke the rule and got along real well. But like my mom says about these things, "We didn't cause the problem, and we can't fix the problem."

She even says that about my old dad because I used to think there was something wrong we did that made him so angry that he went away from us. Sometimes I think I worry so much about what other people think of me because my dad left us, and I don't want to repeat whatever mistake I made. But I was only two when I made that mistake, so how could it have been so bad? I've seen two-year-olds and they can be pretty stubborn, but they can't really help it any more than dogs can stop themselves from barking or birds from flying. But maybe my dad didn't know that. Maybe he thought I was the only two-year-old who wanted what I wanted when I wanted it. My mom tells me not to try and figure it out, but I still wonder about it a lot.

After we eat the cookies, Eddie wants to play video games again, but I must have given my mom a look because she says, "Gee, Eddie, Danny has lots of homework on school nights."

"C'mon, kiddo," Frank says to Eddie. "We'll see more of Danny and his mom when we go ice skating Saturday. Let's leave them to their work."

We walk Eddie and Frank to the door, and then Frank says something pretty normal in an odd way. "I'll tell Marilyn to stop by," but his voice is quiet like something is making him not so sure he should.

After they leave, I ask Mom what's the problem with Marilyn, and she says she doesn't really know. Maybe Marilyn is real busy with Eddie and Carly, or maybe she's shy. We'll meet her someday and see, she smiles.

When we do meet Marilyn, I almost have to laugh to think that Mom said she was shy. Marilyn reminds me of Eddie in a way because she seems so young, and she doesn't really seem to think before she speaks. "I wondered who'd ever buy the Miller's house," she tells my mom. "It's a real project, your old place." Then she smiles like she's said something more like a compliment and waves good-bye. She's tall and kind of pretty, but she looks strange for it being eight in the morning. Marilyn is walking Eddie and Carly to school, but she looks like she's going to the opera. She has this purple knit suit on that's kind of tight and real high heels, and her hair is all in curls on the top of her head, which makes her look even taller. She towers over my mom, and I bet she towers over Frank. It's pretty cold out, but all she's wearing is this suit, and she looks real tan.

"Why was she so dressed up?" I ask my mom in the car.

"Maybe that's what she needs to look like for work," Mom tells me.

"She doesn't work, Mom. Eddie told me."

"Well, some women like to look real nice all the time. Maybe Eddie's mom is one of those fancy women."

"Well, I think you look nicer," I say. "You look like a mom."

4

THE NEXT SATURDAY at eleven we're going ice skating. One thing I like about Mom is how she finds what I need. By Friday this oldish pair of skates has shown up. The black leather looks crackly around the ankles like a broken vase, but Mom had the blades sharpened, and they're seven, just my size. If I ask her where she got them, she'll pretend with her hands like she's doing magic and say, "I just conjured them up." I know that she has in a way. At some time during work, she took a break and raced around to resale stores until she found them. Sometimes I go with her on her "safaris," which can be fun at times and boring at others. Once she needed a certain color shoe to match some dress, and I thought I was going to die and get eaten by worms before she found them. But at other times, it can be real fun. That's where I got my whole game system and some of the games, believe it or not.

You can't imagine what some people call junk. Sometimes I think that a person like Grandma who only buys new things might think that our house looks like one big resale store. We could put tickets on everything and none would say very much money. But I think it's kind of nice how things get another chance at our place. Once Mom brought home this dirty lamp.

It looked so filthy that I couldn't even imagine how light could shine through. "Maybe it's just an artwork," I told her, "a lamp that can't give light." I had seen a show like that somewhere with Aunt Sheila once. But after Mom washed the base and got it a new shade, it was a lamp, all right. I guess you have to use your imagination when you go into these stores. If you can't, you'll be passing up a lot of good things.

So at eleven the doorbell rings and Eddie and his dad are standing there. "Where's the little one?" my mom asks, and Frank tells her that it's someone's birthday today, so she couldn't come along. We take our sweaters and mittens and lock the door behind us. Mom always double-checks the door before we leave. There's no reason not to be safe in the city, she always says, and then we're on our way. I kind of thought I'd sit in the back with Mom, which is what I like to do, but when she tried to climb in the back with me, Frank said that she should sit in the front. He smiled at Mom then, but she looked more nervous than pleased. If Frank was Marilyn instead, Mom wouldn't have hesitated, but she is kind of shy with men, and Frank isn't even a man: he's a dad.

Once Mom dated this guy named Michael who she knew from work, but I hardly even saw them sit near each other when he came to visit. Once I saw him take Mom's hand and kiss it in the kitchen of our apartment, but that's the only time I ever saw them touch. Michael had these bushy eyebrows, which made him look like an owl, and he was from the South so instead of saying the letter W, he said "Double-yuh." I once told him how to say it, but my mom said that was rude.

When we get to skating, we find out some bad news, especially since skating is about twenty minutes from where we live. Usually there is skating right now like Mr. Nova thought, but today there's an ice show for the kids who take lessons.

"We could watch it," my mom suggests, but Eddie is wailing by now and Frank is whispering something to him.

"Eddie is dying to skate," Frank explains, and his face is already a little red, and his eyes, which are this light blue like an Alaskan huskie's, look kind of in pain. They're watery and even bluer. "There's outdoor skating downtown. Let's try that," he says without a chance for us to agree or disagree.

"Is that okay with you?" he says as an afterthought to my mom.

"Fine with us," she smiles. "Danny was set on it, too."

She doesn't tell him how she was probably looking all week in ten places for my new used skates. My mom never brags to other people about what she does, that's for sure. Like when she makes a new card design and then we see it in a store, my mom just says quietly, "Look, Danny. That's mine." She doesn't shout it all over the store like Grandma or Eddie's mom might do. Heck, I might even do that if I was a little famous like my mom.

Which is why I think as I'm writing this that this story about Eddie is really more about me and my mom. Eddie would have just been the kid next door for the rest of my life if it hadn't happened.

What's there to say about Eddie that day expect that we did skate and Eddie was fast and kind of wild. Both of us were wild for a while. We skated as fast as we could and sometimes we bumped into each other hard—on purpose—and fell on the ice and flopped on our backs like we were unconscious. And Eddie liked slamming into the sides like he was a crash test dummy until a guy at the rink told him to quit it. Then my ankles felt kind of nauseated and I had to stop, and when I got back to the bench where my mom and Frank were taking a rest, it looked to me for a second like he was just letting go of her hand.

When we rode home in the car, this is what I remember. Eddie asked Mom if she believed in heaven, and I heard Mom lie for almost the first time. Don't get me wrong, though. Mom won't tell Sheila that her dress looks like it's made of pot holders. She'll say, "Your new dress is really unusual, Sheila," but I don't even count that as lying. But when Eddie asked Mom about heaven, she said, "I think most people go to heaven, Eddie."

"How good do you have to be?" Eddie asked.

"You need to be kind to other people."

"But what if you're bad sometimes?"

"Bad sometimes doesn't count."

"How many times can you be bad?"

"We're only human, Eddie."

"Jesus can forgive you, right?"

"You can act better. There's always that chance."

Now that may not seem so odd to you, but my mom hates religion. She even hates heaven because she thinks that religion causes too many problems in the world. Even in my neighborhood, where a lot of Irish people live, there are problems with religion. Just ask Riley Flowers. He'll tell you how one neighbor who's Irish won't talk to another Irish neighbor because of something that's happening in some other country. But I think my mom was lying for the same reason she does about Aunt Sheila's pot holder dress. Eddie is maybe worried about how he behaves sometimes, so my mom is being kind to Eddie. She understood that Eddie needed heaven. That's kind of creepy to think of now that he's not here anymore.

Eddie's dad, by the way, was real silent, like he's never heard the word *heaven*. That's odd because Eddie went to church with his family. And if they didn't talk about heaven, what did they do there?

5

Two things happened the next week that really didn't have much to do with Eddie at the time that they happened. First, we get a puppy, which is what Mom promised me about a century ago. "First we'll get a house, and then we'll get a dog," she told me when I was about six.

"When will we get a dog?" I asked her a million and a half times.

"When we have a house."

"And when will that be?"

"When I've saved enough money."

"And when will *that* be?"

"It'll be when it is," she always said, but I could tell she was worried or not too hopeful that I'd have a dog in this lifetime.

Now there's the house and there's the little black dog which cries all night and tries to eat dumb things like paper clips off the floor. We have to keep everything super-clean and get these special plugs so Guy—that's what we call him—won't electrocute his little doggy self. And he sometimes misses the paper where he's supposed to pee, and once, just like the old excuse goes, he ate my homework, and I had to do it again. That all sounds kind of annoying, but believe me, there's nothing like getting licked to death by a little puppy that's round and helpless as a real baby. And there's nothing like having him at night when you're sort of tired and he helps you get to sleep.

When Eddie saw the puppy, he nearly went crazy. He must have pet it for about three days straight. "You're going to wear out his fur!" my mom joked.

"Don't you have to ever go home?" I finally asked him.

"Can I take Guy along?"

"Oh, sure," I said with enough exaggeration in my voice for anyone to notice, but then Eddie raises the window and jumps out of it with Guy and I have to chase him all over in the cold before he'll give him back.

That's why Eddie had to ask about heaven, because he's sometimes the most annoying person I know.

The next day we get a call from Marilyn, who can't find Eddie. He sees a tutor today, and the tutor is waiting, and he's not home. She's hoping that he's here. There's Guy dreaming and twitching on the couch, but there's no sight of Eddie. I haven't seen him all day, which is odd. He's always here when he's not there.

About an hour later, we see Frank and Eddie getting out of Frank's car. My mom rushes out to tell Frank that Marilyn had no idea where Eddie was, but before she can say anything, Marilyn is standing about a foot from Frank's car, and she's screaming her lungs out about where he's been and why Frank didn't call. I think it's kind of exciting the way they're both shouting—I've never really seen my mom have a fight like this—but my mom tells me to close the door and leave the family alone. She says some things are private, but if you're out shouting on the street, it can't be private for very long.

The same week we get Guy there's an article in the neighborhood paper about some people who are sending Easter baskets to Northern Ireland and darned if one of them isn't Riley

Flowers. But I'm thinking that the other men in the picture (it's all men) look like pirates from my illustrated *Treasure Island*. It's hard to believe that these tough-looking guys are interested in orphans halfway around the world and work for something called the Green Cross. "Do Irish people have green blood or something?" I ask my mom and show her the picture. She says, "That's odd. It says they're in a fellowship group together, but as long as I've known Riley, I've never seen any of those men or heard of his fellowship group."

"Don't they look bad, Mom, except for Riley?"

"Well, they're probably men who work hard and don't think too much about how they look."

"Who do you think looks best, that guy Michael who used to come over, or Riley Flowers, or Frank Nova?"

"Frank Nova wins hands down."

"Is he handsomer than Alex was?"

"He's nicer, that's for sure," my mom smiles. But all night she's kind of quiet and seems to be thinking hard.

"What's wrong?" I ask her.

"Sundays; taxes; Guy, who's chewing up our whole house; Marilyn, who seems so angry; and that picture of Riley Flowers. It makes me nervous."

"Those guys he's with look mean."

"I've seen nicer-looking pirates," my mom says, like she can just read my mind.

"Isn't it funny how people can look nice and not be nice like Mrs. Canberra, or vice versa."

"Mrs. Canberra was nice for a lunatic. She only put you on trial once, right?"

"We were six years old and she wanted us all to write essays about our behavior. And half the kids couldn't even write yet."

"You could write, Danny. I remember what you said. You

said that children and adults need to behave all the time. That was very clever."

"That's why she put me on trial."

"I thought you did something bad, that's what you told me."

"She told me it was bad and I believed her, but I don't think so anymore."

And then my mom said something I think about a lot now. She said that anything that doesn't kill us makes us stronger, Mrs. Canberra included. I don't think that applies to me anymore. I'm not sure there's any saying that does.

We kind of got used to living in our new house over the next few months. Mom went back to her usual hours at work, and Aunt Sheila came over afternoons sometimes until Mom got home. I walked home by myself from the Hayt School, where things were going okay for being the new kid and all. I'd found a friend at school, a kid named Canyon whose mom was an old hippie, my mom said. Sometimes I'd play at his house after school. We'd usually just play video games or watch TV, but now and then his mom took us somewhere fun. But it had to be educational, too. Once we went all the way to Indiana to see Amish people, and once we went to the aquarium and saw the whales. Lots of people think whales shouldn't live in aquariums, but these guys seemed happy enough there.

Mom and me also saw more of Eddie and Frank, but most of the time the four of us did things together. Every third weekend when Frank was off and Mom wasn't working, we'd go somewhere. That spring we saw the Cubs and the White Sox both, and I was there when Frank Thomas hit a giant home run into the upper deck, and the exploding scoreboard acted like it was the Fourth of July. We could grab handfuls of smoke where we were sitting. We went to the zoo and saw a puppet show about snakes. Sometimes Mom would let Frank just go with Eddie and me somewhere, like when our Little League season started and there were practices about every night.

Instead of having to practice with my mom or my mom and Sheila, which was the absolute worst, Frank would take me and Eddie down to Loyola Park, where we'd catch flies and get pitched to until the sun went down. Frank liked to fool around when he pitched to us. He had a real good arm and good control. Sometimes he'd get funny and start throwing knuckleballs or split-finger fastballs. I'd just shake my head, but Eddie would get super-upset, and Frank would start laughing. He never teased me like that. Maybe it wouldn't be polite, or maybe I just wasn't as easy to tease as Edward Franklin Nova. That was his whole name.

When we were out together, Frank seemed to talk to me more than Eddie. I'm kind of good at talking to grown-ups. Eddie sure wasn't. He'd cross his eyes or pull out his gum and stick it on the car window and act like he didn't have a thing to do with what was being said right to him. Sometimes Frank looked at me a lot, like he was judging me or wondering what he should say next. After a while he started asking me about my mom, like how long she'd been divorced and if I saw my father much and stuff like that. Knowing how Marilyn acted, I couldn't decide if he was interested in my mom or just interested in getting a divorce. I mean, if he still had to see Marilyn a lot and be divorced, it would hardly be worth the effort, so I guess he was trying to learn how divorces work.

That May Frank took me and Eddie on a fishing trip. My mom was supposed to go but at the last minute she got a call from Carol. Carol told my mom that Riley was in some kind of trouble. I asked my mom if she remembered the guys who looked like pirates. Because of that picture, whatever Riley's problem was, was no surprise to me. It's like class pictures. You can just look and see which kids make the trouble. It's usually some big guy in the last row who just jumps out of the photo like even the picture can't contain what's inside him. Sometimes he has googly eyes or sometimes his hair is a mess, but it doesn't have to be. This year it's Peter Kogenas. He looks pretty regular except that he's not looking at the camera, but you should see how he acts. He takes things out of people's desks and is fresh to the teacher and likes to knock other kids down by just butting them with his big fat chest. He makes Eddie look sweet. And it's never a girl who's the class problem. I wonder why that is. Anyway, we were supposed to leave for this campsite on the Kankakee River when my mom got this phone call.

So Mom asked if Frank would mind just taking me along, and he said, "Sure, no problem." Then Eddie and me went to the car, and the two of them talked in the house for a while.

6

I PROBABLY SHOULDN'T say this with what's happened and all, but this weekend was the only time I thought that maybe someone like his dad should knock some sense into Eddie. We're staying in this quiet place where people go to get away from the city where it's loud and crowded and maybe dangerous, and what does Eddie do all weekend? He runs around screaming and throws rocks at people's tents and scares this old dog with not too much of a coat of fur and long pinkish nipples on her stomach and falls down some rocks and disappears for about an hour and throws my new cap in the river. All this before we've even tried to fish. Frank's in the river up to his knees trying to get back my White Sox hat and Eddie's laughing like it's the funniest thing he's ever seen. And I say to Eddie, "How did a nice man like your dad get a son like you?"

Usually Eddie just laughs at just about anything, but this time he's really pissed at me and his eyes get all tiny like he's shooting death rays with them, and he takes my arm with all his power and twists it behind my back and says, "Shut up, faggot."

By now my baseball cap's somewhere downriver, maybe in Kentucky, and Frank is running toward us at full speed. This is not a very relaxing weekend for poor Frank Nova. He's already started shouting from way far away. I hear him, but I don't really pay attention because Eddie and me are pounding on each other real good by now. I'm sitting on Eddie's chest, but not for long because he starts biting my arm, and I'm about to jump off him when I feel Frank tugging at me.

"What the hell is going on, you two?" Frank shouts, and he holds me tight by one wrist and holds Eddie by his shirt with his other hand.

"Danny called me a faggot," Eddie is whining, which is just about the biggest lie I've ever heard.

"I think you have me confused with you, Eddie!" I shout.

"But you said something mean. He said something, Dad."

"What did you say?" Frank asks me pretty quietly like he's real tired and maybe wished he had a different life altogether.

"I said I was sorry that you have a son like Eddie."

"Why would you say that, Danny?"

"Because he's always causing trouble. He's always ruining our time. We haven't even got to fish yet because of him."

"The three of us are here to have a good time together, Danny. It's your time and my time and Eddie's time. Now let's try to make it work out, okay? And don't worry about your cap. I'll get you a new one," he says in this voice that big people use to sound like they're the boss when maybe they aren't.

And then he hugs me. And then he hugs Eddie. Eddie squirms all over and says something under his breath like "Okay, Dad." I stand there thinking two things. I'm not his kid even if I am nicer. And the other thing I'm saying to myself is that I'd really like to go home right now.

By that evening we haven't caught a thing, and I'm thinking so much about going home that I start to cry at supper. Frank has cooked us hamburgers and given us chips and juice packs, but I can tell Frank is miserable, freezing in his wet pants and shoes. I think only Eddie, who's throwing some kind of nuts or seeds at the tree nearby and won't come to eat, is having any fun.

So Frank looks at me with maybe some pity in his eyes or maybe he's making fun of me a little and says, "You need to see your mom, right, Danny?" His eyes look funny like maybe he's going to cry, too.

"Yeah," I say, and we pack up and get into the car and ride back real quietly. Thank God my mom is home when we knock on the door, and I don't have to stay at Eddie's or see him for even one more minute. And though my mom is happy to see me—she hugs me and everything—I think for a minute that she's maybe even happier to see Frank.

As soon as Frank leaves, I can't help it. I just start crying, and my mom asks me if I'm hurt. "Just tired," I guess, I tell her. Maybe tomorrow I'll feel less awful, and I won't have to tell her every single disappointing thing that happened. But then Mom starts telling me about how Riley Flowers is maybe in trouble with the government, but all he was doing was being generous. And I start crying again because I guess I feel sorry for myself. I think I'm kind of like Riley Flowers and Eddie's like those pirate guys in the photo. Some people are always try- ing to make the world better and others are always working real hard to make it worse.

At times like this I wish I had a dad because my mom doesn't want me to tell her the real sad things I sometimes think about. She's never said that, but she gets so upset when I tell her anything sad that I just keep quiet mainly. I think dads don't care as much if you're sad about something. Maybe it's because they love you even more. Or maybe they love you less. I can't decide.

(A note to Dr. Pockross. You told me to be honest, so what

I really wanted to write was that I thought Frank should kill Eddie that weekend. I didn't want to write *kill,* though, so I said he should have knocked some sense into him. But I know from talking to my mom and watching TV a lot that violence doesn't solve anything. So maybe writing *kill* would be better because you'd know that I was just exaggerating, but with what's happened, I can't very well say that either.)

I've been reading all that I've written so far, and I think maybe whoever is reading this will think I'm trying to make Eddie sound worse than he was so I won't seem so bad. But even if Eddie was the worst kid on earth, I'd still be bad for what I did. And even if I was the nicest kid on earth before it happened, you still can't really call me nice anymore, can you? Sometimes I say the words. I say, *I killed Eddie Nova,* and wherever I am, I feel so sick that I start shivering even if it's warm in the room. And the room gets slanty and my eyes make everything shine like it's such a hot day that the world is slowly melting. And I think about this, too. My mom finally has a house that she loves, and now we have to move. Who could live in that house anymore? And who would want to buy a house where someone got killed? It's like I've ruined everything. There's a curse on things, and there's no way to change that.

Sometimes I imagine the whole afternoon again and do you know what I do first? I take the bow back to Eddie's house, and in my imagination, Frank is home, and I ask him if knows that Eddie is running around the neighborhood with his compound bow, and Frank thanks me and locks it up. But sometimes I imagine this instead. Frank comes over that afternoon instead of Eddie and he seems real mad at me. Maybe he knows that later that day I'm going to kill his son, so before that can happen, Frank shoots me. And then my mother comes home and sees me lying on the ground and Frank standing over me, and she slaps Frank real hard.

I don't know what this means, but you're a psychiatrist, Dr. Pockross, so maybe you do.

7

I THINK MY mom and Frank started kissing right after that first fishing trip. It made me real nervous to see him bending down and kissing her right on her lips. The first time I saw them kiss, they were in his garage, and Mom had just gotten me a new bike. Frank was helping her fix the seat, which was a little too tall for me. The bike was green and had a banana seat and fifteen gears. My old bike was red and had no gears and was about big enough for Carly to ride if she got some training wheels.

So I'm running back and forth with Guy and throwing him sticks, and out of the corner of my eye, I see them standing real close like they're whispering. I look more carefully, and I see that what they're really doing is kissing like people do at weddings.

I run all the way to the corner with Guy and while I'm running, I'm kind of squinting or closing my eyes because I don't really want to see anyone. If I saw Eddie or Carly or Frank's wife, what would I say to them? Or if I saw Carol, who lives right across from the park, what would I tell her? But she's probably over at Riley's house because Riley can't have the job he does working for the government and help those men make Easter baskets that go to Ireland at the same time. Don't ask me why. Riley says he might retire and move back to Ireland. His voice sounds all shaky when he says that, like he's angry at the people who are interfering with his life. Maybe he's just saying that for revenge because I don't think that Riley could leave Carol, or my mom, or even me.

I'm wondering more about my mom and Frank Nova. Have they kissed before? Maybe each time Eddie and me play in my room, they're kissing somewhere. Maybe they've kissed in the kitchen and front room, too. Maybe they have an obsession like I saw in a movie about these two pretty old people—the guy was even bald—who gave up everything they had to live together in some place that looked like Hawaii or Mexico. And when they got there, they couldn't stop fighting, and he finally killed her and took off in a boat with all their money, and the movie was over.

Boy, I think, Marilyn better not see them. She's about the meanest lady I've ever met. Once she slapped Carly for dropping her bubbles all over the place. Carly is only five and bubbles get awfully slimy after you open them, so what's the big deal?

It's easy to understand why Frank would like my mom more. I like her much more than Marilyn. She's more normal and calm and everything, and her eyes even look quiet and soft, not like Marilyn's crazy eyes that are always rolling all over the place like she's lost something or wants to be somewhere else. But I keep thinking this. Eddie's dad is kissing my mom. The father of Eddie Nova and the husband of Marilyn Nova is kissing my mom. There's a reason for everything, my mom once told me, but I can't think of a good reason for this.

By the way, Riley Flowers did go to Ireland but for only two weeks. And guess what? Aunt Carol went with him, and they brought me lots of presents when they got back. They got me an itchy sweater knit by fishermen and marbles and a book of Irish fairy tales and a shillelagh—that's a walking stick. And they brought my mom this pretty shawl and lots of different teas.

When they got back, Riley said he was going to work at the church full-time getting their records organized better and seeing that their spring rummage sale really runs well. It's not that important a job, I don't think, but Riley sounded like he was president of a new company. And Carol seemed relieved. She has this funny rubbery face that can look pretty or ugly depending on her mood. Before they left for Ireland, there were a lot of days when Carol was ugly, but now that Riley has a new job and she got to see Ireland and get away with him, she looks pretty most of the time.

Almost as soon as my mom started kissing Frank Nova, she started looking prettier. Not like she changed that much. It just seemed her face was shinier or her eyes were brighter. I kept staring at her to try and figure out what part of her got improved. I studied her lips for a while, thinking that maybe they had become different, but my mom has a little mouth with neat lips and nothing was different there. So I began to examine her all the time. Sometimes she'd ask me what I was looking at, but I never said. I just concentrated until I decided what was different. Her forehead wasn't worried anymore. That's what I finally decided.

8

JUST ABOUT THE time that school ended in June, Frank decided it was time to try fishing again. He'd take Eddie and me away for a nice weekend, and this time my mom would come along, too. We'd sleep on a boat, my mom told me, as she showed me her latest resale store prize, a tiny tent that kids might play in when they're five or six years old. "For the yard," she said, "this summer." I had no idea where Mom thought a kid as big as me might fit in it. And I had this funny picture in my mind all of a sudden. Maybe Mom thinks I'm an elf or a midget although I'm almost as tall as she is, five foot two. Sometimes she tells me that I'm going to be as big as my dad, six two, but then she always adds the punch line, "You'll never be as big a jerk."

When I told her the tent was too small, she was already busy showing me other things—four sailors' hats, one for each of the crew, she said, a fancy new fishing rod for me, and a cooler for keeping drinks. She told me that I'd better bring my swimming trunks. I noticed Mom had another bag that wasn't from her usual stores, Vagabonds, or Upscale Resale, or The White Elephant Shop. It was from Marshall Fields, and it had a new bathing suit in it. I guess Mom was planning to do some swimming this weekend, and she didn't want Frank to see her in the ratty old stretched-out thing she usually wears. She's had her old blue baggy bathing suit with the falling-off trim since I can remember, so I guess it's about time that she brings home a new one. I wonder if she'll really wear this new thing at all—it's pretty little—red and black striped—or whether she'll just hide it under her usual weekend gear—jeans and running shoes and a baggy long shirt.

It turns out that Frank has borrowed his friend's boat. Why do so many firemen have boats anyway? Maybe they want to get as far away from fire as possible during their time off. Water in hoses might remind them of fire, but not water that's all stretched out into a lake. Maybe lifeguards take vacations in burning buildings, I suddenly think. The four times Frank took us out on boats, they all belonged to his firemen friends and one boat was prettier than the next.

This one was a twenty-nine-foot sailboat by the name of "Honey" with beautiful old wood and some pearly-looking stuff stuck into the walls and tan leather seats. It had a fancy bar with a lock and a galley and a shower and four little beds with green blankets. I don't think that Mom really liked the boat as much as I did because under the picture of "Honey," there was this cartoony-looking woman with lots of lipstick and big hips and boobs. She was wearing a curvy bathing suit and high heels. When Mom saw that, she just kind of turned her head because this cartoon woman would make Mom look pretty sick in her new suit.

It sure was a more peaceful trip than my first one with Frank. We didn't fish as much as we swam and ate and fooled around. Most of the first day, Frank dropped his anchor here and there. Eddie and I put on our life jackets and dove right off the front of the boat into the water. Lake Michigan water is cold all year round, and this June water was no exception. We couldn't stay in more than ten minutes before we'd feel numb and achy and have to pull ourselves out freezing and shivering. But the boat had a warm shower underneath. We'd huddle in there and get all warm again. Mom made us wait until our goose bumps went away, but then we'd jump right in again and swim some more.

Eddie behaved pretty good all weekend. It seemed that Mom could calm him down just by talking to him softly sometimes. During the trip about the only thing he did wrong was throw one of my shirts overboard. Frank put this big long stick with a hook that you use to save drowning people into the water and got it right back for me. And all Mom said was "That was Danny's clean shirt for tomorrow, Eddie." And Eddie didn't laugh or scream or act like he was skating up the walls without a skateboard. He and Mom just sat there looking sad like they'd broken each other's hearts.

I don't know if Mom and Frank kissed that weekend or not. I didn't see them kiss, but Eddie and me were gone lots of the time and Frank seemed pretty happy and so did Mom whenever I noticed them at all. People say it's pretty romantic to be on a boat after the sun goes down and you're just rocking in place like you're in a big peaceful cradle. And the air smells new and your skin is fresh from the mist. So I'd guess that after Eddie and me finally turned off our Gameboys and went to bed that maybe they sat on the deck and got a blanket from underneath so they wouldn't be cold. Maybe they unlocked that bar and had a drink though my mom doesn't like brown liquor. She likes wine and beer and maybe vodka, or is it gin? Probably they just started talking, but suddenly they might have been kissing or having sex. I wondered if Marilyn thought about that while we were away, but you couldn't really apply regular rules to Marilyn. Maybe she cared and maybe she didn't.

I also know that by the last day, Sunday, Mom was wearing her bathing suit all over the place. She wore it while we ate lunch. She wore it while she sailed the boat. Sometimes Frank had to help her, and she seemed pretty comfortable when he put his hand over hers to straighten out the sail. And she didn't seem to mind it either when she got herself caught on a hook, and Frank reached just under her suit in back by her thigh and unattached her. And once when I guess they thought no one was looking, Frank blew her a kiss from across the deck, and guess what Mom did? She caught it and put it down her top.

Finally, toward the end of summer, Frank took me and Eddie camping and fishing again without Mom. This time it was like an official club. We had three meetings before we left—Frank and Eddie and me, and we all had jobs to do while we were away. Mom got me all this stuff to take, including a Swiss army knife. I didn't think she'd ever let me have a knife. When I was little, I didn't own a single toy gun or anything, but she said a knife was practical for this trip and gave me one with nail trimmers and a scissors and a corkscrew and a magnifying glass on it. I felt like James Bond when I got into bed and played with that thing. But sometimes when I was on that trip, I sort of felt left out. I kept thinking that I sure could use a dad like Frank, but that probably wouldn't ever happen because, well, there's all those people—Eddie and Carly and Marilyn between him and me and Mom. I imagined what it would be like if Frank tucked me in at night or if I got sick, he could carry me upstairs and just put me in bed like Mom used to do before I got too big. I'd watch him and Eddie just talking about nothing and feel kind of sad about things. Some people are lucky. For no reason they get the good fathers and other people like me for no reason either get the lousy ones.

Mom always says that people feel jealous because they envy you, and that weekend I knew what she meant, envying Eddie so much for having Frank. When he leaned down and said good night to us, I felt his beard, and I sort of remembered feeling that with someone else, but I didn't know who. Maybe it was Riley, but his face is pretty smooth, so it might have been Dad when I was just small and he was living at home. It's odd to imagine that I can still remember how my dad's beard felt when I know so little else about him. I don't even know his favorite baseball team or what TV shows he likes. Maybe there are other things I can remember about him, but I guess what happens now has to help you with what you remember from before. Now is a hint about then, but sometimes I wonder why we have to carry so many people around inside of us at all. It would be a lot easier on us if we could just close our eyes and see blackness or think of all the stars up there floating around that don't even know who we are.

At night I kept thinking this: I bet Mom and I think about the same thing before we go to bed. I bet we both think about Frank Nova. But I never tell Mom what I'm thinking about at night. She'd be too shocked if she knew.

9

ONCE GUY GOT lost, and I think that if this story ended differently, the thing that happened with Eddie wouldn't have happened because I wouldn't have known Eddie anymore.

In early October of the year when Guy was still a puppy, somehow our gate got unlocked. We have two gates to our house, one in front and one in back. The front one is always locked so that people can't walk down our gangway and sneak into our yard. Not that our yard is so special, but there is a toolshed with a lawn mower and shovels and rakes. Also there are opossum in the toolshed, and once in the summer Guy almost caught one. It was a young opossum, which made it look better than opossum usually do. It was pinker and rounder and kind of looked like a stuffed animal. So this pink cuddly possum is lying in our yard looking to all the world like it's dead, and Mom calls Guy in. He's reluctant to leave at first—maybe he wants to eat the thing though all he's had up to this point in his life is hard dry food. So we get Guy inside and we turn around to take care of the dead animal. Mom says she'll bury it by the peonies, but guess what? It isn't dead at all. It was playing possum, pretending it was dead so that Guy would go away. And believe it or not, it fooled all of us—Mom and me and even Guy, who was back at his bowl eating his puppy chow while the thing was sneaking away. People are real smart, I know that, but animals with their instincts and all can trick us any day.

It was a real cold day for early October, which can be a beautiful time of the year. Sometimes we have Indian summer then, and it gets real hot for a few days and your feet swell up in your shoes and people even go to the beach. By October the water is about the warmest it'll ever be, so even without lifeguards, you enjoy this chance. But this year the cold came early and seemed to be staying.

That day we left the gate to the alleyway open, and Guy must have slipped out when we sent him outside to go. That's what we did so we wouldn't have to stand in that jagged wind and freeze. Five or ten minutes after I let him out, I go into the yard to bring him inside, and he's not there. First I stand like a dummy staring at the yard like I'm just missing him in front of my eyes. But Guy is sixty pounds by now and a little hard to miss.

I come to my senses and search up and down the alley and onto the next street, but there's no sign of Guy. I call his name again and again. I go racing back home and tell my mom that Guy is missing, and now we're both outside without our coats calling his name. We decide to split up, each taking a block. Mom races toward Broadway, the big street near our house, and I head toward Glenwood.

As I run, I think of what dogs know. Some seem to come equipped with a sense about cars. They only walk when the light is green, and they watch for turning drivers and everything. But it's the other dogs I'm mainly thinking about, the ones who don't have the first clue about how to be alone. I'd guess Guy is one of those that starts to cross when the wheels of a car are a few inches away or stops in the middle of the street to smell something that takes his fancy. When they see strangers, they approach with a look of dumb hope on their faces as if they're asking, "Are you my person?" It always makes me sick to see lost dogs like that, the ones who aren't streetwise. My mom once said that maybe the streetwise dogs have been dogs longer, maybe in another life. She sort of believes that we were all alive before. Sometimes she jokes about being a British soldier during World War Two, and I can tell that she's kind of serious. These dogs with second or third lives have already practiced being dogs for fifteen or thirty years, but I know for sure that this is Guy's first turn.

After my mom and I each looked about four blocks away, we happened to meet on the street and decided we should come home for now. "He'll turn up," Mom said with a little smile. But she didn't want to look at me because her nose was running. It was clear she'd been crying. We waited three or four hours for him to show up. We stood in the picture window silent and sad. I said things to myself like, "Guy will show up when I count to seventy." I even made bargains like saying in my head that I'd always keep my room clean and take out the garbage if Guy comes now. I wondered if Mom was bargaining, too.

When he didn't show up, we finally got to work again. We had a photo we took this summer of Guy and me in the yard near the maple tree. We used the photo on a sign that offered a reward and ran to the Kinko's and spent sixty-nine cents apiece on color photocopies. We posted them on different corners of the blocks around us. Mom said she'd take one to the grocery the next morning, and I said that I'd hand them out at school on Monday.

She said we should also call the animal shelter that night. She added real quickly that Guy had a name tag and would be found soon when she saw the look I had on my face imagining the place. I once read a story of how a man somewhere, I think Mississippi, lost his collie. The same day the animal shelter found it, they put the dog to sleep because it looked sick to them. When the man came to get his dog, they apologized for their mistake. By now the man was so angry that he got a shotgun and fired some bullets into the windows of the shelter. Now the man is in jail and the collie is dead. That's some story, I kept thinking when I heard it. You wake up one morning and your life is fine. By that night, you've been given a whole new bad life, or maybe you've given it to yourself.

We were both pretty depressed that night. Mom had made bowtie spaghetti salad with tuna and peas, but we're not eating or talking and the TV isn't on. We're sitting on the couch and the loveseat like we're out visiting some strangers who don't know how to speak.

Almost twelve hours have passed since Guy was last seen when the doorbell rings. When I see that it's Eddie, I wonder why he didn't come through the window, but then I see that he's standing there with Guy, and Guy looks normal like he's done nothing wrong.

"Here's your dog," Eddie smiles.

"You found him?" I ask, and I'm ready to kiss Eddie at this point.

"Eddie's a hero," Mom says as she welcomes Guy into her arms. Guy, meanwhile, is slobbering all over us like he's been around the world and is happy to be home.

"He came over this morning," Eddie continues. "He was at our door when my mom went out to the store."

"So you just brought him in and kept him all day? You didn't think of asking us if we were missing Guy?"

"How did I know you were home?"

Something in my chest is making me feel that with all this anger I could take Eddie by the arm, swing him over my head, and toss him into deep space. "But did you even try?" I shout in a lunatic voice I hardly recognize.

"Well, we're happy to have Guy back," my mom says like a politician. "But the next time," she adds, "will you tell us where he is?"

"Sure," Eddie smiles. It's no concern of his that we've been crazy all day.

After that happened, I ran this through my mind again and again. "You can't trust Eddie," I said to myself like the lyrics to a song. I was falling asleep that night with Guy on my bed and my heart pounding like some crazy, broken motor. It was only when I petted Guy that I felt a little calmer.

But while I'm in bed, I hear Mom talking on the phone. She's making small talk and her voice sounds babyish, half like she's talking to a child and half like she is a child. I can't figure out who it might be. I know it's not Sheila or Carol or Riley or my grandma. When Mom talks to Riley, she always sounds polite but kind of bored, and when she talks to her mother she sounds kind of like a siren if a voice can also be a siren. Then I hear her mention Guy and say, "So you'll tell Eddie?" and realize she's talking to Frank. But if she's talking to Frank, why doesn't she sound like she does when I've done something really stupid? Frank should know how bad it was that Eddie kept Guy. For a minute I feel like shouting at my mom, but I know I'll just fall asleep and feel worse by tomorrow.

And by the next day I did feel worse. I woke up thinking that I could never be friends with Eddie again. Usually my mom doesn't care who my friends are. If I want to see Canyon, fine. If I want to see Todd, fine. She's not the kind of mom who bothers me about who I should like or why I don't like this or that one. She never makes me have plans if I just want to stay at home and build something out of ropes in the basement or watch cartoons all day Saturday in my pajamas. Once she helped explain to Todd's mom that I didn't want to play when he did. She said later that it was kind of rude, but she did what I asked and didn't bother me much about it. But I knew she'd care this time. If I wouldn't see Eddie, how could she ever see Frank?

So here I am in this new house with my own room and my own dog. And Mom and I are happier than ever because we have all these normal things finally. It's not like we're fancy or anything or rich, but we're comfortable. That's what Mom calls it when I ask her if we're rich or poor. And I think of an old easy chair that everyone likes to sit in when I think of our lives. But then there's Frank and Eddie Nova. There's a game where you say, "He went to Jupiter" and then the other kid has to rhyme with you: "He went to Jupiter to get much stupider." "He went to Mars to buy some candy bars." And the big joke comes with "He went to Venus." Believe me, from then on I would have been happy to send the Novas just about anywhere in the galaxy.

10

IT WASN'T LIKE Eddie and I were always enemies. Sometimes we had fun together, like the time Mom and I went shopping with Marilyn, Carly, and Eddie. I was kind of surprised that we were going anywhere with Marilyn, but I guess she called Mom and made a plan with her one weekend that Frank was working. You see, Marilyn could drive but she didn't like to drive in the city. She said it made her nervous. I wonder what she was really afraid of. Maybe she'd read about car-jackings. I heard of one where a pregnant lady lost her car with her other kid still strapped in it. Later the kid was found asleep at some hardware store in a mall, but they never found her car. Or maybe Marilyn thought that driving Eddie and Carly around all the time was too much for her by herself. Whatever the reason, she called and asked if Mom could drive her to the Lincoln Town Mall. She said we could play video games there and maybe have lunch after she'd finished shopping.

Mom was pretty quiet on the ride there, kind of like she was surprised at where and why she was going. She had her hands at ten and two on the steering wheel, which is what she always tells me about driving. She won't do anything dumb that I've ever seen. She's a defensive driver, she says. Even if someone else does something real stupid, like makes a U-turn right in front of her, Mom won't let herself get upset. She has a good driver's certificate from the secretary of state right in her wallet behind her license.

Marilyn is asking her all kinds of questions about her job. Mom is telling her how she's often given an idea for a greeting card and then she develops the artwork. Marilyn makes some kind of joke about needing a special card for Frank. I can't see Mom's face, but I'm wondering how it looks right now. Then Marilyn goes on to explain, right in front of Eddie and me and Carly, who's combing her mermaid doll's blue shiny hair with this huge pink comb, that she and Frank don't much enjoy each other's company. Maybe my mom used to talk this way about my dad when I was just little, but I kind of doubt my mom would tell strangers. That's what my mom is to Marilyn, a stranger, really. I wonder if Marilyn knows that Frank and my mom are a little more than friends. Maybe she's giving my mom a message. Maybe she's saying that it doesn't matter in the least to her. I also wonder what Eddie and Carly must think. What do they know about their parents already? Will this be news? Or maybe Marilyn acts like my grandma, who thinks kids are deaf and dumb and says just about anything in front of me if she feels like it. Once she said, "He's kind of scrawny for his age," right in front of me, and my mom turned all red on my behalf.

I think I should repeat exactly what Marilyn said at this point because I found it hard to believe she was saying it at all. Maybe if I just write down the words, like she said them, you'll be convinced about what I was hearing because I know that people sometimes think that kids make things up or don't understand exactly what's being said. But here is exactly how it went with Marilyn.

MARILYN: We just don't please each other anymore.

MOM: That's too bad.

MARILYN: It's too bad for Frank, but it's not too bad for me.

MOM: (kind of quietly) Why?

MARILYN: Because it's all a joke, Nancy. We fell in love when we were seventeen. Kids came along, and Jesus, we're almost in our forties now. And I can't even guess what it's all supposed to mean. (The words sound serious, but she sounded kind of perky just then, not sad at all. That's the funny thing about Marilyn. Her face never looked the way you'd expect it to.)

MOM: Some friends of mine see a marriage counselor. I could get his name for you.

MARILYN: The Pope and Joyce Brothers together couldn't help us, Nancy.

MOM: (Silence.)

MARILYN: I mean we don't have anything to fix. We just live in the same house, God knows why.

MOM: (Silence.)

MARILYN: Sometimes I wish he'd go away. You know, he goes out for cigarettes and never comes back. Men do that all the time.

MOM: My husband did a version of that.

MARILYN: You got lucky, huh?

We get to the mall and Marilyn lines up at the token machine and feeds it bills. She gives each of us kids about a hundred tokens for the video games. My mom says that's too much for me to have and is trying to give some back to Marilyn, but Marilyn just waves her off, which is what she'd like to do to Frank. My mom tells me to watch Carly, which I think is strange because Marilyn doesn't tell Eddie anything about her, and she's only five.

We must have been playing for an hour before someone came back, and when someone did, it was Mom. She told us that she'd take us to lunch while Marilyn was having her face done at Carsons.

"She does that all the time," Eddie shrugged.

"Someday I'm going to be the makeup lady, and I'll do Mom's face," Carly said. That's about all Carly said all day.

But I'd have to say that this was one of the nicer days I had with Eddie. We were about equally good at the games, so it was fun to play Streetfighter and Mortal Kombat II until the fourth round even if I did finally lose. The pizza Mom ordered for us tasted real good and was shaped like a dinosaur, and Eddie acted pretty normal all through lunch. When Marilyn joined us, she said she wasn't hungry. She just ordered herself a beer and looked across the room at herself in the big mirrored window behind the salad bar. The interesting thing about Eddie is that he seems to know when to stop causing trouble. Maybe he understands the bigger picture. It's like he knew that his mom was the one with the trouble in her that day, so his trouble just kind of fell away.

I began to wonder that day if he simply behaves better when his mom is around. Some kids are like that. I know that Todd used to be much sillier before his dad got home. His dad was born in Beijing and doesn't think that kids should act very funny. My mom says there was a cultural revolution when his dad was a little boy, and all kinds of strange things happened, like if you were wearing glasses, they'd make you work on a farm, and if you worked on a farm, you'd be forced to move to the city. People would tell on you if you had a pet or something fun in your apartment, and groups of old people would come and take all your fun things away, kind of like ten of my grandmas showing up at once and reporting us to the police. I'd fight to keep Guy, I know that. But back to Marilyn. If she was my mom, I'd be real careful.

First there are her nails, which are so long they kind of curve over the tips of her fingers. They're painted a color that looks like dark chocolate mixed with a few cherries. Then there's the hair, which makes her about four or six inches taller. Then there's the makeup, which is usually pretty heavy, like she's going to be in a play. And on this particular day, the makeup lady had put some dark green glittery stuff on her eyelids and outlined her lips with a different color than her lips had inside them. Her mouth looked like it was ready to lip-sync without her even granting it permission. I tell you, if she was my mother, I'd stay out of her way. If you didn't, I bet you would have nightmares all night long.

When we got home, Mom told me that Carly had wet her pants at the game room. I asked Mom how she knew.

"When I picked her up, I felt it," Mom said.

"Why didn't she tell us she had to go?"

"Maybe no one cares when she does tell them."

"Maybe," I said.

"That's pretty sad, huh?" Mom asked.

Mom and me both shook our heads at the same time. The more we learned about this family, the bigger mess it seemed to be.

I decided to ask my mom a question. I asked her if Frank was a bad father because Marilyn's such a bad mother. I mean, maybe he could have made Marilyn act better or something.

"I think Frank tries his best," Mom said.

I saw that Mom wasn't going to agree with me, so instead of arguing with her, I just dropped it right there.

11

SOMETIMES AT SCHOOL we'd play this game when we did our writing assignments. First, we'd tell a story from our point of view. Then we'd choose someone else in the story and tell it from theirs. I started to wonder that day at the mall what Marilyn's story would be. Probably she would have said that she had a real great time with her kids. She wouldn't notice that Carly looked so lost when she got left with us that she wet her pants. She probably wouldn't notice that her makeup made her look like a clown or that she never fed her kids lunch but made my mom do it. "I had a wonderful day," she'd probably say, which is why I think so much about what people do or don't know.

How could my mom, for instance, who's so careful about everything and thoughtful and concerned, have imagined for a minute that I didn't notice what was happening right under my nose with Frank? I knew that at some point my mom started leaving late at night after I was supposed to be asleep. Usually if Mom is going to leave me at home for even a few minutes, she makes so many plans that you think she's going to Asia or Africa. She writes down three adults' numbers and the doctor's number. She shows me what food is ready and reminds me not to use the stove. She checks the doors and gates and even the windows to see that they're all closed. She tells me exactly the amount of time she'll be away and that I shouldn't answer the door while she's out. She kisses me good-bye like maybe it's our last moment together. I once saw a movie called *Dr. Zhivago* where these two people who loved each other an awful lot kept getting separated by wars and stuff, and I tell you, that actress was no more sincere than my mom when she says good-bye to me and goes to the store.

But now it was all new rules. I'd lie in bed for about an hour, and then I'd hear a lot of rustling and stomping upstairs in her room because she was changing clothes. I'd hear water pouring in the bathroom upstairs while she got herself ready. Then I'd hear her steps on the stairs, and then the door would open and shut ever so lightly. Sometimes I jumped out of bed at that point and watched her get into her car and drive away. I guess she was going to meet Frank somewhere, probably a bar or restaurant.

It was kind of bad that I knew where she was going. I'd lie in bed and picture the place they'd meet. I saw them sitting in that funny way that people do when they're in love. They crowd in on one side of the booth when there's a perfectly good seat opposite. Then they whisper to each other and carry on and even feed each other little pieces of their dinners like they're two little creatures in the woods in a Disney movie. That's what my mom and Frank Nova were probably doing at the moment. Usually my mom would be back by about two in the morning. And I have to thank her for one thing. She never stayed out all night or made me really worry about what would happen next because I do tend to exaggerate some. I worried about school the next morning, if I should just go if she didn't come home and how I would get my lunch money. I worried about Mom, too. I mean what if they were drinking and then she drove home and crashed? But she always came home, and I always had lunch money in the morning.

Around the same time I began to wonder about what happened when my mom sent me to Carol's for the night. I pictured Frank Nova sitting in our front room with all the shades and curtains down like they're spies. Maybe that's why Mom was always checking the windows. She didn't want Eddie climbing into mine just when Frank put his arms around her or she touched his hair and they began kissing. Once when I was at Carol's, I called my mom hoping that Frank would be there. I don't know what it would prove if he was there when the phone rang, but it made me happy to picture them all surprised, maybe even red in the face, because the world was interrupting them. The time that I called, though, Frank must have already gone or not come yet. I woke up my mom with the call, and her voice sounded real tiny, like she was a little girl having a bad dream, and she told me that she was glad I'd called and gave the phone kisses and wished me good night. That's why I could never stay mad at her for long, not even after she started sneaking around with Frank. She's always good to me no matter what.

Still, I wonder sometimes why Mom didn't warn me more about the bow. I mean, she warns me about so many things. She tells me to wash my hands before I eat and cross only at corners on the way to school. She tells me to keep my lunch money in my pocket, not right on my desk where other kids can see it and get greedy. She tells me to brush up and down and to massage my gums gently with the toothbrush. She tells me to keep my toys nice because someday they may be worth something, even the junk that comes in Happy Meals from MacDonald's. She tells me never to run on the deck of a boat, never to go to the lake when it's frozen and walk on it, never to touch a big papery round-looking thing outside because it could be a hornet's nest. She tells me not to ever say "My mom's not home" when someone calls, even if she isn't. Once she told me when we were going to swim on vacation that in some rivers in Germany or somewhere, people can get bugs in their brains from the water. She tells me that earwigs don't really climb in your ears, but I once watched an African show about pygmies, and they do sleep with their heads off the ground to protect against some kind of insect. She told me that the cartoons were silly, that dinosaurs and people never lived on earth together, that the most a caveman would have to fear would be a saber-toothed tiger or a woolly mammoth, which sounds awful enough. She tells me not to talk to strangers but also not to hate homeless people because most can't help it and are drunk or crazy. She tells me who the good guys and bad guys are when politicians debate although she sometimes says that both guys are jerks. She tells me not to eat while I'm running because I could choke. She tells me it's fine to listen to her old records but to put them away exactly how I found them. She tells me that people were prejudiced against Nat King Cole who sounds like such a gentleman when he sings. She tells me not to say swear words to people even if other boys do, and she asks me which swear words I know. I tell her that she taught me to say *shit* when I was very little because she always says shit when she drops something. I don't tell her that I know *jackoff* and *motherfucker*.

She tells me to wait a few minutes before I drink water from our faucets because the pipes are old and maybe they have lead or rust in them. She tells me to take an umbrella even if it's not supposed to rain because you never know about weather in Chicago, but if I'm walking to school, I just hide it in the bushes. Sometimes I lose umbrellas on purpose. She tells me not even to pretend that I'm hitting Guy because he'll become afraid of our hands if I do. She tells me to be nice to Eddie even when it's hard to be because Eddie has a problem about being too active. She doesn't tell me much about my dad, which is what I sometimes want to know. Like did he take me to the park and stuff. Did he get me a balloon? What names did he call me? She tells me yes and yes, but she doesn't remember the names.

With all the things she tells me, you'd think she'd say more about hunting. But she's never been hunting herself and probably doesn't know the first thing to tell me. That's why I had to rely on Frank Nova for everything here, and Mom couldn't help me at all. To tell you the truth, I was real surprised that Mom let me go in the first place. She hates weapons even in video games, and she thinks that it's sort of stupid to chase after animals when you're not even hungry and there are stores on every corner. I mean she wouldn't let me swim in a river where bugs get in your brains, so why would she let me hunt? But once I heard Grandma tell her that I'll become a sissy if I'm with Mom so much. Maybe she's thinking about that when she tells me that Frank is going to teach Eddie and me how to hunt. Who ever expected this, I'm asking myself, at the same time she's saying that Frank has signed me up for a hunting safety course this very weekend. I remind her that she wanted me to clean my room, but she says I can do that Sunday night.

The plan is that we'll stay overnight in Waukegan because we're set to hunt in Wisconsin, and because Eddie and me are under fifteen, we have to take a hunting safety course that lasts six hours, three each day. Now I've had sex education in school since fourth grade and I kind of figure that the hunting class may be the same bad idea as sex education. My mom and I disagree on this point, I'm pretty sure.

She sounded real pleased that I was going to take the sex course. She said it would answer lots of questions for me, and she was really happy when she heard that one day the boys would be in a group by themselves. She told me years ago how people get babies, but I think that certain things I learned in the course would have been hard for her to explain. Wet dreams, for example. She's not capable of having a wet dream, so how is she going to tell me all about it? Kids who have moms and dads maybe don't need to learn this in school.

I guess we need to learn about wet dreams. Some of us may have them in sixth grade, but some of the other issues like safe sex—I mean I was ten. I still had a little boy's body. I wasn't about to have any kind of sex with anyone, so why did I have to think about it?

This is how I felt about this hunting safety course. If you need to catch your food, you should be required to do it safely so you don't shoot yourself or someone else. I heard about a lady in the East somewhere who was shot in her yard by hunters while she was hanging out the wash. One stupid guy saw her moving in her own yard and thought she was a deer. Now it sounds like he could have used a hunting safety class, but what about me? I didn't want to hunt and kill an animal any more than I wanted what happened to Eddie later to happen. Nobody asked me my opinion though. Mom just said that I was going to Wisconsin to learn about hunting like everyone did that in November. It was like all my friends did it. She made it sound as regular as grown-ups going to grocery shop or to work or to vote.

Even before I went for the course, I'd already decided a few things. I wasn't even going to try to shoot an animal no matter what they taught me and no matter what they told me to do. Let Frank shoot all the deer in the forest if he liked. I'd just be quiet and close my eyes and wait for the day to end. And it made me pretty happy to think about Eddie and how he can't sit still. I don't think that deer are attracted to moving objects. I figured that we'd get to the woods and Eddie would blow it as usual. All during my first class while they were showing us films of people hunting with rifles and compound bows, sitting still as corpses while they waited for their prey, I thought of how quiet you had to be up in your tree stand. Even a twig breaking or some leaf falling can tip off a deer that someone is after him. It isn't possible for Eddie to cooperate for this, I kept thinking to myself. And I was smiling at all the opportunities we'd miss, just sitting in the class with a big private grin on my face. If someone looked, he would have thought I couldn't wait to go hunting, but I was picturing the back of Frank's van empty and us coming home from Wisconsin with Frank real quiet all the way because it hadn't been his dream weekend. I thought of our first fishing trip, what a disaster that was, and I felt reassured.

But then I felt sorry for Frank, too, and my mom because I saw in the film that good compound bows cost two or three hundred dollars. I wanted to tell my mom not to bother. But then I heard about Frank's connection. He had a friend, another fireman, of course, with a hunting cabin near the Wisconsin Dells, and his friend had all kinds of equipment, so for now we wouldn't need to buy hardly a thing—just licenses and camouflage gear. It would be kind of cool to own camouflage gear and sneak around my house like I'm Rambo. Maybe I could wear camouflage and follow Mom and Frank some night and see where they're really going.

I didn't know what to think about my mom and Frank Nova. Were they in love? Maybe if she'd go so far as to send me hunting, they were. If she just liked him or wanted to be with him now and then, I don't think I'd have been sitting in that class, and I don't think anything that has happened would have.

So in the two classes, which went pretty quickly, we learned some rules and regulations. We learned about tagging deer even before we field dressed them and displaying the tag when we drove them back to the city or wherever. If you didn't display that little tag, you could lose almost $2,000 and the chance to hunt again for three years. We learned never to carry deer through the woods but to drag them because some crazy guy might think a deer that's being carried is still alive and shoot you instead as you walk with it. We learned to be sure of our target, never to shoot until we were certain it was a deer. We were also told to be sure of what was behind the target because if we miss, Mr. Jenkins or whoever won't like to feel an arrow in his big fat butt. They showed a cartoon about that, and I thought it was pretty funny then, but I can't laugh at anything of that sort now.

They showed us the actual mechanics of compound bows and said someone my size would need one with twenty-five pounds of pull. An adult's bow has forty-five or fifty pounds of pull, but once the arrow is released, a man's bow or a boy's bow shoots just as strong. Never aim your bow at another person, not even when you're joking, is another thing they said. I remember thinking, right. Who is dumb enough to do that? For a minute it went through my head that maybe Eddie is dumb enough. It turned out that we were both dumb enough.

Each day after the class, Frank came to meet us with this big happy smile on his face like our lives as men were just beginning. He'd say corny things to us like, "Are you men ready for lunch?"

"Yeah, I'll have the kid's meal," I laughed, but Frank didn't want to hear my jokes. He wanted to hear what we had learned. As usual, Eddie had nothing to say, and I had to be the reporter on the scene. I'd tell him everything I'd remember, word for word, and he'd say, "Is that right, Eddie?" like I was trying to trick him.

"No, I'm lying," I sort of joked, but Frank didn't like jokes when kids are sort of rude. He was less patient than my mom that way. I can say about anything to her, and she'll never remind me that she's the grown-up. Frank said things like that all the time. "I'm the grown-up," this six-foot man with gray hair is telling me. Maybe he wasn't as sure about it as he should have been. Maybe because his wife doesn't like to listen to him, it's important that everyone else does.

Sometimes I think back to that time and wonder where Eddie's head was during all this preparation. Maybe he was daydreaming. Maybe he didn't want to hunt any more than I did. I don't remember him ever saying that he wanted to go hunting. I don't remember Frank asking either of us. When we finally went hunting about a month later, Eddie broke some of the rules we learned in hunting class. Sometimes I thought that maybe Eddie is freer than me. Maybe he just tells his dad how he feels by being so annoying. Maybe he'd rather hang around with Marilyn and Carly playing video games all day, only Frank keeps dragging him along. Maybe I was more willing than Eddie to be cooperative with Frank for the sake of my mom. Maybe I shouldn't have been.

IT'S DECEMBER FIRST when we finally get around to deer hunting, and it's as cold as it gets. Not only can I see my breath as steam, I can see it as mist hanging in the air. It doesn't get much colder than this, but Frank says we'll be all right if we just follow his instructions. Under our camouflage suits we have to wear sweaters plus our winter coats. On our hands we have these camouflage gloves that really don't fit because they're a men's size. Under those gloves I have regular gloves, which I imagine I'll wear most of the time. I'll just save those camouflage gloves for when there is a deer in the vicinity. On our heads we have watch caps and hoods and then the camouflage hood over that. We all look about twice our size, and Eddie really takes advantage of the situation. He's doing Frankenstein impressions all the way up to the Dells. He's talking as stiffly as he's moving his hands. He sounds like a real dumb guy with a low voice.

We had to wait so long to hunt because bow season and rifle season are two different times. Around Thanksgiving, Frank told us, is rifle season, and the hunting officials tell you to stay in your house because the woods are crawling with hunters. If you go out, you never wear white because it's white-tailed deer they're after, and you always wear an orange suit to distinguish you from everything else. Bow hunters in their camouflage wouldn't stand a chance during hunting season. We'd be prey, too.

We leave the night before because you want to be in your tree stands at dawn. On the way up we see herds of deer just like cows standing here and there, and I wonder why Frank just doesn't get out of the car, take his bow, and get this over with. More than that, I wonder what Mom is going to do all weekend without me and Frank, but she'll manage. We arrive late Friday night, and it's so dark that I can't even make out the cabin when Frank first pulls in. When my eyes finally adjust, I'm already inside the cabin, which isn't much to look at. Frank's fireman friend has it nice for a place where guys stay. He has some warm checkered blankets on the beds and lots of wood for the stove and fireplace and a dark braided rug, and in the kitchen he has these black iron skillets and pots hanging and a few little plaques that you'd see at a grandma's house, only these don't say things grandmas would want to hang on their walls. One says, "Put the tits in the oven," only tits is crossed out and over it there's the word *buns*. And there are little flowers around it that look like someone sewed them on. I wonder if this fireman guy actually made the thing. I once saw a football player on TV who knits in his spare time, so anything is possible. And there's also a clock that's made out of a toilet seat. Eddie laughs when he sees it. In fact, only Eddie's in a good mood right now. Frank looks sleepy, and for all that I'm wearing, I still don't really feel comfortable. I feel like I'm walking around wrapped in an iron-coated sleeping bag.

Frank's brought food from home, and he opens a can and warms it. He brings us big bowls of chili and mugs of warm chocolate milk before it's time to go to bed. He tells us to sleep in our clothes because this cabin won't be as warm as our normal houses. You can say that for sure. When I went to pee, I thought it might freeze on the way to the toilet. Then he tucks us both in and musses our hair and mutters something about tomorrow and deer. Soon, he's lying still in his bed, and in about a minute, shorter than it takes me to get used to the lights being out, he's snoring away like he has no cares in the world. All I'm thinking about is how tomorrow I may have to stop a heart.

I never thought anything would be like it turned out to be the next day. First of all, the woods are freezing, and the land crackles under us as we walk. It sounds as if our feet are cracking everything we step on, like we're giants on this fragile ground. I can't imagine that a single deer would stay in this part of Wisconsin with the racket that we're making. I see a few black birds, I don't really know their type, but I notice they're not afraid of us. Here we come with all our gear and our feet making a racket, and they just stand there anyway. Maybe their little yellow eyes have watched hunters for a long time, and they know they're in no danger from men with compound bows. We also see these wild turkeys, which are awkward and look like cartoon animals. They make so much noise as they wobble about that I wonder why any deer, other than a deaf one, might want to stay in this woods.

I'm carrying an Oneida compound bow, a Tomcat EXP. Last night I read this catalog, and it says it grows along with a young shooter's ability and strength. I don't feel like I have much of either as I hold it in my hand. It's funny how much I'm thinking of it. I've carried baseball bats and tennis rackets and brooms to help my mom and hockey sticks for roller hockey, but there's something way different about carrying an Oneida compound bow. It's dressed in camouflage, too, and I keep feeling like this is a dream in which I've been made to hold something I'd never have a use for in real life. You know, like those dreams where you're walking into a school building and someone hands you a giant ticking clock.

Eddie is being strangely quiet for once, maybe because it's so cold, but as soon as Frank has it all arranged and Eddie gets into his tree, which is the farthest one into the woods, the racket begins. What's Eddie doing up there, I wonder, skinning the bark off the tree? I keep hearing this sound like flesh being ripped, but maybe I'm only imagining I heard it now because that's the sound I heard when Frank dressed the deer.

I'm second farthest into the woods. Maybe Frank figures that he'll get the shot before either of us has a chance to screw things up, but that's not what he's told us. We're supposed to be ready if anything comes his way. He'll get first crack, he says, but then we'll have to be ready to back him up 'cause what if he misses? As cold as it is today, I can't imagine not missing. My fingers feel like they're going to break when I bend them, and I can see where little icy places are collecting on the scarf that I'm wearing over my mouth. If my mom was here, she wouldn't let me stay in this tree for ten minutes, but here I am rubbing my hands and my nose is running like mad, and even my eyeballs feel like they're about to chip in their sockets.

When I look down from where I'm sitting, I can see why Frank chose this part of the woods. There are deer tracks all over the place frozen into the ground. When we just got here, I didn't notice that, but then it was still real dark. Now that the sun is coming up, there's more to see, and where Frank has led us begins to make sense to me.

Before we got up in our stands, Frank said we'll spend the morning here, and then we'll see how we feel, so I figure that if a deer doesn't come along pretty soon, it'll be safe until tomorrow when we repeat this at dawn. What will we do the rest of the day in that freezing cabin? I saw some board games in the corner, but who wants to play Risk when you can't feel your fingers or toes? Maybe Frank'll take us to a Holiday Inn and we'll swim the rest of the day and then curl up under blankets and watch HBO. Usually *Mrs. Doubtfire* is on around every ten minutes.

Just when I'm thinking this, my heart starts racing because I hear what's coming down the path. Either a pretty noisy hunter is headed in this direction or it's a deer. Almost as fast as I hear it, I see it, and damned if this doe isn't on deer hunter's salary or something. She's just standing there looking around a little past Frank's tree but not quite near enough to mine. I imagine Frank up there setting the bow and peering through the sight. And just as I'm going through the actions that Frank would take for the shot, I hear the steel blade make a thwacking sound, and I see the deer fall right there. Like someone who's fainted. My own heart feels like it might tear itself into pieces and break open as I race down my tree and head for the fallen deer.

Frank is already standing there examining what he's done, and when he sees me, he puts a big grin on his face like it's the best thing that's ever happened. Eddie must be asleep or something. He hasn't even stirred with all this commotion. There's something you feel when you've just seen an animal get killed. It's like you're inside the animal looking out at the world and you're dead, too. I wonder if Frank feels this or if it's just me.

"This doe made it easy," Frank says to me softly, like we're complimenting good behavior on the part of the deer.

"She just stood there," I say, and I guess I sound sad.

"In her tracks."

"Why do you suppose she did that?"

"Maybe it was her time," Frank said, and I thought about

how people say things like that a lot. I remembered my mom telling me about when my grandfather died, how everyone acted like it was meant to be, but she felt broken in two. Maybe they're the normal ones and my mom and me are extra sensitive. I feel like the deer's glassy eyes are targeting mine as they stare into the sky.

I guess it took me a while to get here because the deer isn't twitching or bleeding anymore. You can see from its glazed look that it's dead, period, and I guess that's the one good thing about arrows. If you strike the deer in the right place, it's a quick death. If you hit it, say, in the shoulder, the deer will just run around the woods for the rest of its life with an arrow stuck there. I saw a photo of a deer like that at our hunting safety lessons. The whole woods might be filled with near misses, I suddenly thought while Frank and me are standing over this deer for the longest time without saying anything more. Maybe he can't believe it either. It's not like he hunts every day of his life. He's bending down and touching the deer here and there with the palm of his camouflage glove. Sometimes it looks like he's massaging it. It's kind of a skinny young deer. I guess he's checking for a heartbeat, but you can tell by the deer's dead face that what Frank's doing isn't necessary.

Suddenly it dawns on him that Eddie hasn't come down from his perch, and he goes down the path a ways in search of his son, who has probably managed to do himself some damage up in that tree. I'm left alone with the body, which is giving off steam because it's so cold, and I'm kind of hoping that the deer will leap up and make its way back out of the woods, the way that opossum did once in our yard.

When Eddie gets to the deer, he's noisy as usual. He's shouting and jumping around and acting like he's at a hockey game. He puts his finger on the deer's nose, and that's when I most want the deer to do its *Night of the Living Dead* impression. Instead, Frank gives Eddie the tag that goes on the doe. Eddie ties the tag around the doe's ear like a kind of bracelet. Frank's number shows clearly on the bright orange tag.

The next thing you have to do, you need a strong stomach for. Frank has a hunting knife and makes a slit in the deer's throat. Blood oozes out of her neck onto the steaming ground, and I think of pictures of saints I've seen at the Art Institute. One of the lady saints even had her breasts cut off. But this deer is another kind of saint, I'm thinking, because she didn't really want to be one. She's more innocent than a saint because she was in the wrong place at the wrong time. Plus, I keep imagining a human body because the deer is the size of a woman or an older boy. In fact, with its slightly distant gaze, the deer reminds me of my mother when she's looking out the window and thinking about who knows what. This deer's eyes are pointed toward the trees, where she'd like to be hidden, I'm sure. And her coat is shiny and healthy. She must be pretty young to look so good. I suddenly start thinking that she is probably the prettiest, healthiest dead deer in the whole damn forest.

It's much better to think of that than to watch what Frank is about to do. Taking his hunting knife again, he rips open the deer's belly and cleans it out like you do a fish. Only the deer is much larger than any fish I've seen, so now there's a heart and a liver and a steaming pile of intestines just under the tree that might fit into maybe a hundred buckets, and Frank is telling us that we have a problem because the ground is too hard to bury them properly. I think about our hunting safety film and how it all looked so easy—smiling men shooting deer, tagging them, burying entrails. I feel like I'm in a horror movie more than anything right now. Even the smell is horror movie stuff and the endless steam that separates living things from the rest of the dead world. Eddie says we can just leave the intestines there, but I can see that Frank is considering a different solution.

He is grabbing handfuls of frosty dead leaves from the ground near trees, and he is telling us to do the same. I run down the path that Eddie just came up, and if my chest didn't hurt from running in this cold, I might just have thought of continuing all day and night. My body is bursting with some sort of a sick excitement like I've done something terrible and gotten away with it. Maybe I think the deer police should arrest me, but I just run and run like this for a long time until my eyes are teary and I'm not really seeing where I'm going, at which point I hit a tree trunk and graze the only part of my cheek that shows. It doesn't really sting any more than the rest of my exposed skin, so I don't think about it much. Still, I stand around for a while and jump up and down to stay warm and listen to the sound my gloves make when I rub them together. "Chush, chush, chush" is the only noise in the woods.

Lots of time later, I come back toward Frank and Eddie with my fistfuls of junk I picked off the forest floor, but by the time I get there, they have already buried the entrails in this big pile of leaves. I'm thinking an awful lot about leaves and not much about the doe or her intestines. I guess it's keeping me busy to see the big fat dictionary where Mom presses leaves every fall and to think how red a leaf can be. But all of the leaves we've found are getting spider-webby and thin, and there isn't much color except for pale yellows and browns. By spring everything we left here will be dust, and the deer that Frank is beginning to drag toward his van will be the hunting story that maybe I'll someday tell my children.

I already know I'm not going to say much to my mother. She

can't even stand a show where people kill a rattlesnake or an alligator. I'll just tell her to ask Frank if she wants to know what happened. Maybe he can account better for all the things we're supposed to feel. I can only account for a kind of dull sadness that is expanding through me like all the emptiness of winter.

When we got home from hunting, my mom wanted to know what had happened to my face. I told her I had run into a tree and not much else about the whole damn day. Since we came home a day early, Frank still had the night off, so he came back into our house later that night and laughed and drank beer with Mom while I was supposed to be asleep in bed. They even took out Mom's old 45 records and played one that Mom and I usually sing together. "It's My Party and I'll Cry If I Want To" has always been her favorite. Well, there they were singing their lungs out, and no one except me was thinking about what we'd done to that deer.

Frank said he'd hang the deer carcass in his garage some-where. I bet the ride home and hanging in that cold garage would have made it look deader still. I kind of felt like slipping out and seeing it one last time, and maybe if they had fallen asleep before me I would have. I felt closer to the doe than any living thing, I figured, so maybe a visit would cheer me up.

The next morning, Frank was taking it to some place in Niles where it would be made into deer sausage and deer steaks. I promised myself that I would never eat meat again when I heard that news, and for about ten days I kept my promise. I wondered what they would do with its head, its skin, and its hooves. I wondered about its eyeballs the most because they seemed to have the most life left in them. Thank God that Frank had no plans to hang the head on the wall.

Probably Marilyn wouldn't have liked that at all or Carly either.

When my mom asked me how I had liked hunting, I just mumbled answers like I'd turned into Eddie, and Mom looked real sad, like she knew what a bad idea it had been, but who can take back what's already happened? If I could take things back, we'd move in next to some crabby old people who never said hello to us. Then our lives could have stayed the same forever.

13

IT WAS THE coldest winter in forty years. Every morning that my mom went outside to go to work, her car wouldn't start, so Frank told her to leave her car in his garage. Every morning that Mom drove me to school, I looked at the empty space where the deer used to hang. I imagined it still there sometimes, season after season, until some other family bought the house and discovered it. Sometimes I dreamed about the deer. Usually I wouldn't be hunting. The deer would show up in places I didn't imagine, like my classroom or my closet. Once it was in the bathtub, but that was a funny dream because it was also talking to me and smiling. When I thought about that deer, I sometimes wondered if how cold it was this winter wasn't connected. I mean people think that astronauts change the weather. Why can't dead deer?

Staring into the garage so much, I saw things that I bet nobody expected me to notice. Most of Frank's trophies from high school were in the garage in the cold. I bet if you touched the little man holding the football on his player of the year award, the gold-plated hand would have broken right off. Either Marilyn didn't win awards or she kept hers in the house. I saw a box of old shoes including baby shoes and huge galoshes. I saw sleds and lawn mowers and a bowling ball that was colored like a tangerine.

That winter Lake Michigan was frozen farther out than I ever remembered, and some boats in the Midwest, boats that haul things that cities need, like salt for the streets and extra car radiators, were stuck in canals that usually don't freeze. I don't know why I was keeping track of everything that wasn't working right. Six homeless men froze one night on Lower Wacker Drive and it became a major scandal for the city. The mayor himself walked around for a few days and invited all the street people to come to some new shelters he just had opened. My mom says most of the homeless people can't accept a favor because they're mentally ill and wouldn't be on the street otherwise. All of the people the mayor spoke to looked like frozen residents of another more seedy galaxy. The mayor's face was redder than usual. He wore silly earmuffs under his hat. When I was little, my mom said I used to call earmuffs ear muffins.

In that garage I bet I was looking for something that would give me a clue to what I was looking for. While I laid in bed and listened to news and weather reports until one in the morning, Mom and Frank whispered and sometimes laughed. The way they laughed together made a sound like music, but it was when their talking stopped completely, and I knew they were in the house that I always thought of this winter story.

There was a Polish lady, ninety or so years old, living all by herself on the Near West Side. Her neighborhood had some older Polish people like herself and lots of Puerto Ricans. Mom and I used to go to some resale stores over there because people with money had started to move in, too, and sometimes they thought that junk was anything two years old or more. We got some real nice things for the house there, like this table that looks like a treasure chest where I keep all my games.

Anyway, this woman's husband had died a long time ago, and she never had any children. She owned her house but not much else, and she didn't have money to keep it up anymore. When her heat went off during the worst week of all the cold, she went down to the basement to look at the damage. While she was in the room, she must have fallen and not been able to get up. A few days later, neighbors remembered they hadn't seen her in a long time, and when they came to check on her, they found her still breathing, frozen to the basement floor in a praying position.

This was a typical Chicago story that winter. Somehow the lady managed to live, but I kept thinking of her all alone down there, knees frozen. I imagined that she was the loneliest person in the world. I thought maybe I should call her and take her to lunch or something. Sometimes I disagreed with myself. I thought that maybe I was the loneliest person. After all, who was lying in bed alone night after night listening to my mom whispering? Who was listening to music and laughter? At least the old lady had God to talk to.

Around the time that the lady froze to the floor and lived, Riley and Carol came to dinner. I was real happy they were coming because my mom had been seeing less of them since Frank got into our lives. I really liked Carol because she was always happy to see me. Usually she brought me something like a comic book or word search game, but more important, she had lots of time to talk to me. I'd tell her about what I was doing at school. Like I'd say that I had grown crystals for the science fair, and she'd get real interested and ask me lots of questions, not stupid adult kind of questions that show someone doesn't really care at all, but smart questions like a friend might ask if the friend was a grown-up who knew a lot but wanted to know more.

And Riley was even better. Ever since I found out that Riley Flowers, this really round, bald guy was doing something kind of illegal, I just wanted to be around him and study him. I mean, I was doing something kind of illegal, too. I knew way too much about my mom and Frank. Maybe my mom is really bad at hiding things, or maybe I'm just good at sniffing things out. I thought that maybe I'd become a detective when I was older. There must be lots of couples like my mom and Frank, and someone like Marilyn might want to know more. I could be the guy that finds out more. I could follow them around and take some photos, and I could record things that their kids said about how they acted.

Well, I thought that night I could tell Riley Flowers that I wanted to be a detective and see what he thought, so when Carol, who had brought my mom daffodils wrapped in lots of paper so they wouldn't freeze and me a seahorse growing kit was in the kitchen helping my mom with the roast, I asked Riley Flowers if he had ever known a detective.

"I know a detective in Ireland," he said. Almost all his stories involved Ireland. It's like the only life he lived was there, but he hasn't lived there for twenty-five years or more.

"Really?"

"His name is Brandy Boggs and he's a sneaky fellow. Once I watched him sit all night listening to a man at a bar who was just a stranger. I was visiting from the States, and I wondered why Brandy was so interested in this big stupid fellow and his stories instead of me. Turns out he wanted to hear one point about a soccer match. This one point was involved in an investigation he was making of a certain soccer player who was maybe betting against his own team at games. That's a rotten thing to do, Danny, but I don't suppose you'd ever try it. You seem like a pretty honest fella to me. It takes patience to be a detective, Danny, but you seem like a mighty patient sort."

When Riley talked he massaged the top of his bald head, and sometimes I felt like touching it and seeing if it was getting warm.

"You bet," I said, and then felt kind of awkward, so I followed it with a story of my own. "Sometimes I listen at night to my mom. I'm supposed to be asleep but even when there's no sound down there, I can tell if she's alone or not."

Riley was quiet for a while, like he was deciding what to do next. He ran his fingers through the reddish-white fringe surrounding his bald spot. He needed a haircut.

I could almost see Riley's face struggling to decide. Not like in movies when an angel and devil sit on your shoulder and fight for your soul. More like someone looking in a shop window and figuring out what he should buy. Should he go on with the thing I'd just said, or should he avoid it because I wasn't supposed to know anything about it? I could understand if he just avoided it, but I hoped he wouldn't. If he avoided it, I supposed I'd still like Riley Flowers, but I wouldn't like him in the same way. If he would just make a signal, I'd think that Riley Flowers was the coolest adult in the world.

"It must be hard for you, Danny, Nancy's new relationship," he said softly. He was rubbing his fingers together like he was cold or nervous.

That's all he said, but I felt like crying after he said that. Instead, I smiled at Riley, but there were tears in my eyes because I finally felt I had someone I could talk to. Riley lived really close to me. I could walk through my alley and down the next block and turn right at the corner by Senn High School, and I'd be there. Riley's house is a really funny place because he's divorced and lives like a kid. Whatever he wants is wherever he leaves it. If he's decided to read all of the books by Mark Twain, they're stacked on the living room floor next to this big toolbox because he's also decided to fix his gas fireplace. If he's eaten spaghetti in the last few months, you know because the bottle of store-bought sauce is washed out and has a few dried leaves in it. If he's going to grow tomatoes that spring, he has rows of tomato seeds growing in little brown cardboard pots. If his dog, Michael, decides to knock over the tomatoes, Riley just lets them fall. If his cat, Stump, who has three legs, wants to sit on the Twain books, she does for a few days without Riley saying a thing. And now that he works full-time at the church, his house has gotten even stranger. He has church stuff all over, outdated bulletins and broken signs and even old collection plates. I can't imagine what he does with them. Maybe Stump and Michael use them as food dishes or maybe he's just collecting old collection plates. Anyway, I felt like I'd accomplished something that Riley knew that I knew. Now I was like the frozen lady. Somebody had come to thaw me out.

14

I COULD JUST tell about our lives for the next few months, but that seems like cheating considering what I still have to explain. I grew two inches that winter and Mom said that maybe I was starting my growth spurt. If I was, I'd be getting armpit hair and everything. Those two inches seemed to just arrive one day. I looked in the mirror, suddenly seemed taller, asked her to measure me, and that was the end of the story. What if I said that I suddenly started growing so fast that people on the street could watch me grow? Each day I came home from school in clothes that no longer fit me. My low-riding baggy-legged jeans were up around my calves. My toes burst through my shoes and proved a real hazard on those cold walks home. My head brushed the tops of branches, and I had to wear protective goggles like Kareem Abdul Jabbar. If this kept up until spring, I'd be covered in leaves and bird nests. How would you know? How will you even know if what I'm about to tell you really happened in the way that I'm going to tell it?

That's the strange thing about what I'm about to tell you. What happened took it away from me. It would be easier to just make up something than tell you about that afternoon. When things are just happening like any day in your life, you don't pay much attention, and after they turn out so terrible, maybe you don't want to know. So the part I'm about to tell, the part you really want to hear, seems a little out of my reach.

Once I got an assignment in fourth grade. I had to write an essay on whether we should allow illegal aliens to stay in our country or send them away. My mom got real angry when she saw that assignment. She wondered what any nine-year-old had thought about the subject. Well, this is kind of the same. I know it happened, and I know I've thought about it almost all the time since, but I wasn't expecting it to happen. I didn't have an opinion until I was forced to have one. And by the time I was forced to have one, Eddie was dead. My opinion is that I killed Eddie. I know how I did it. I know how the bow was in my hand, how I must have released the arrow. I know all the details, but I still don't know what they mean.

You know because I told you that I'm a pretty good detective. I can put a lot of things together, not even events but sounds or even whispers and reach a conclusion, so maybe you think I should do better with this. Maybe you think that I'm playing a game with you when I say I don't know what they mean. For example, if I hear a man's voice in the house, I know that Frank is over, especially if I'm supposed to be asleep. If we get something about Ireland, I know that Riley sent it to me. If Guy growls at night, I know he is having a bad dream. Probably the Doberman down the street is straining on his leash and trying to chase Guy like he does now and then. So how can someone who knows so much suddenly know so little? I've taken you up to here, and now I'm going to leave you helpless, kind of like my mom did when she sent me to hunt with Frank. I'll try to do my best to explain everything, but if I still don't really know why it happened, and if all I know is how it happened, how can I tell you more?

It was a Wednesday in late February. It was Leap Year Day,

a day that only happens every four years. If you are sixteen and born on that day, you're technically four years old right now. If you're eighty, you're twenty and so on. It was another frigid day, the kind that makes your skin crack at the corners of your mouth and causes pretty red sunsets late in the afternoon.

I had gone to school and studied the usual things, only school had been pretty special because it was my day to present my science project on growing crystals. I'd left them there all weekend by themselves, and when I looked on Wednesday, they were still growing. I ate lunch in the cafeteria, which I usually like because they have this way of scrunching down the toast against the cheese like they've been joined forever, and it really tastes great. I had a good day because the class cheered for my project when I explained it and wanted to touch everything.

I got home at around three-thirty, which is my usual time, and I let Guy out into the yard. I watched him through the window and wondered if he noticed seeing his breath like people do as I ate a green banana with hardly any taste and some vanilla wafers. I called my mom at work and told her I was home. That's something I had to do every day. She asked about my crystal project and I told her that maybe I'd be a scientist when I grow up. She asked me if I was going to give up on being a detective and I said, "Not quite yet, ma'am."

I started watching TV, a *Duck Tales* episode about a very rich duck. It really bored me because when the doorbell rang around four o'clock I was sleeping in my chair, and it startled me. That's something I should tell you. Since I got these new curtains that my mom likes and these white shutters that hang on the inside, Eddie didn't come through the window anymore. So the doorbell rang around four and I knew it was Eddie, but I asked just the same because I had promised my mom I'd always ask. It's hard to believe that anyone who wanted to kill me, a murderous stranger, would bother ringing the bell, but a promise is a promise. Even when Mom comes home around five-thirty and I hear her key in the door, I say, "Who is it?" and she says, "A robber." It's a joke between us. Even without asking, I knew it was Eddie because only Eddie came over at exactly four.

Eddie was standing there in his Bears parka and his usual fat black gloves, but I didn't really see his hands yet because he was holding something behind his back. Even from being outside for a minute, the skin under his eyes was already pink and wounded from the cold.

I opened the door and saw that he was carrying the bow that Frank had bought him for Christmas after we went hunting. It wasn't enough that the hunting cabin had bows to use. Frank had to give Eddie his own bow that very first month he'd been hunting. I guess the bow was supposed to tell Eddie that for as many falls as they were father and son, they'd go to Wisconsin and kill a deer. I guess the garage would have had a new deer hanging in it every December if Eddie hadn't brought over a bow that Wednesday.

So I let Eddie in and asked him about it.

"I just thought I'd bring it," he said. He laid it aside with his coat and his gloves, all of which he tossed on the floor in the hallway in a big heap. If my mom was home, she'd have me hang up Eddie's stuff, but since she was still at work, I just left it all right there. I know she likes the house neat, and I thought it would be neat by five-thirty.

Eddie suggested that we walk Guy, and as soon as Guy heard those words, even though he'd just been out, he was whimpering and hanging around his leash. If he could, he would have hooked it on himself, the words made him so excited. I knew how the walk would work. Eddie would hook the leash on Guy. Eddie would walk Guy. If Guy pooped on the sidewalk, I'd pick it up with the scooper and put it in a bag. Eddie would never do that. At some point in the walk, Eddie would do something nasty to me or to Guy. Like he'd walk where the only solid footing was and leave me or the dog to climb some huge pile of dirty snow. Or he'd get the poor dog so tangled in his leash that Guy would fall over, and I'd have to help unwind it and say something mean to Eddie to make him remember that Guy was my dog and he was being a jerk.

But neither of those things happened that day. Eddie seemed calm, and our walk was pretty quiet and quick because it was so damn cold. I remember how dark it already seemed at four in the afternoon like all the color had gone out of the world after the sun went down. I wondered what it would be like to be an animal that doesn't see any colors. Pretty depressing, I decided. I didn't say much to Eddie about those kinds of ideas. Eddie didn't care about interesting conversation, and I think I know why. Eddie had two parents, so he could just be a kid and think about whatever. I had to be better company than Eddie and come through for my mom, so I was always thinking up these clever things to say. I didn't know if I cared or not. It had just become a habit.

We walked Guy all around the high school, and I considered asking Eddie if he'd like to visit Riley, who lived right there. But then there was Guy, and it would have felt like imposing to bring my dog for a visit when he already had his own dog and cat. Not that Riley would have minded, but maybe Eddie would have said something about his house being messy or his hair being funny or his cat having three legs, so we just circled the school and went home. When we talked outside that day, it created major clouds of breath between us.

By the time we got home it was about four-thirty, and there was still an hour before my mom would be back. I had homework to do, but I never did homework with Eddie around. I suggested we watch TV. *Baywatch* is on then, and it's kind of pleasant to see pictures of somewhere where it's warm on a day like that one, but Eddie said no.

It was around then that he walked into the hallway and picked up the bow and started goofing off. At first he didn't say anything while he held it. He just swung it over his head like he was doing a baton routine, only the thing was heavy and uneven, so he looked like a spastic baton twirler. We both were laughing at that and he was getting more and more awkward with it just to be funny, but when I motioned for Eddie to give me the thing, his eyes got mean-looking. His face, which was all freckly, flushed. He started pointing the thing all over the place. He pointed it at the couch and at me, but before I could say anything he was telling Guy to come. Eddie was holding the thing just like he was ready to bag a deer.

Now Guy just lives in the house and plays all kinds of games with me. Sometimes we play war and I throw bunched-up towels at him and pretend they're grenades, so he didn't seem too disturbed that Eddie was pointing a weapon at him. It bothered me plenty, though, and I told Eddie to put it down and he said no and cocked the bow. I told Eddie that that wasn't funny, and he laughed real loud, this big fake laugh that you could probably hear way next door. His eyes looked almost like he was getting a fever, and I thought for a minute that acting bad was a disease to Eddie. Maybe he just couldn't help himself, and maybe there was no cure. So I took Guy up to my mom's room and closed the bedroom door. I knew Guy would be upset and whine and paw at the doorknob, but I figured that was the best place for him.

All the way up to the room Eddie followed me with the bow, and coming back, he stuck one end of the thing in my back like it was a rifle and he was the sheriff. I was really becoming annoyed by now and thought of asking Eddie to leave. Instead of telling Eddie to leave (and he probably wouldn't have listened anyway), I was feeling more and more upset as he poked me with the thing. I turned around real quick right then like I was going to grab it from him, and Eddie ran into the front room and stood looking through the sight at me. I was standing near the TV, and he was right near the front door like he was blocking it, like he was saying that he lived here, not me. The house was his, the dog was his, I was his, and maybe even my mother was his. It kind of reminded me of Frank, how he must think of my mother. I thought for a few seconds how if Frank and my mom got married, Eddie and I would be related. He'd be about the worst brother in history I was thinking when Eddie engaged the arrow and pretended that he was going to shoot me.

Well, that really made me angry, so I ran at him and called him an asshole and grabbed for the thing. I got it right away from him because, I guess, Eddie never expected me to rush at him like that. He just expected everyone to take it because he was Eddie. Well, maybe because he had almost been shooting it already, the arrow was engaged, so when I turned on him and pretended I was going to shoot him instead, the arrow fired out. We were no more than four feet apart.

When I saw it enter his chest right near the pocket on his Catholic school shirt, I knew something terrible had happened. First Eddie was thrown back by the force of the thing being so close to him. He fell against the door behind him and I heard his body make a sick crashing thud. About as soon as he hit the door, Eddie staggered forward toward me moving his lips as if his plan was to tell me a secret. Before he got to me, I had somehow gotten him into my arms and was laying him on the floor. At first I didn't see too much blood and thought maybe he was just playing, but when I looked at myself and under him at what was flowing out on the rug, I knew. I also knew from the way his eyes, which were looking into my face almost with a question right after he got shot, looked glazed and distant now, like they didn't care. I knew from movies and things to feel for a pulse, but now I couldn't find one in his wrist or in his neck or anywhere.

It's hard to tell what happened next because what I remember isn't what happened next. I remember hiding under our porch in the bitter cold. But I didn't feel the cold. I didn't feel a thing. It was like I was just another piece of icy junk under there, where things got left because they were too big for the storage area or because they weren't good enough to bring in for the winter. Under the porch, there was a folded-up woven lawn chair frozen from the cold. I remember staring at the chair until the white and salmon colors mixed together and for a second my mind was still. Another way to say it is that for a second my mind had a focus and wasn't completely empty as it had felt since what happened inside. I thought a few times about getting up and moving from there. I thought that maybe I should go to Riley's for some reason. I never thought about going to Frank and Marilyn's or calling an ambulance. I knew it was too late for Eddie.

I guess deep down I was thinking about myself, that I needed to hide somewhere but I never left the place under the porch, not even when I saw my mother's car. Instead, I called her, but my voice wasn't right. I could only make a sick whisper like I was talking from inside a giant dark seashell. At first she didn't see me, so I was whispering toward her legs, but then she finally did and her face turned real white and some-how, seeing her face that way, got me feeling hysterical instead of dead myself.

"Danny, why are you under there?" she asked. Her voice was angry at me.

I couldn't tell her because the words wouldn't come out, so I told her to come under the porch with me, and she did and gave me a hug, but her eyes never left my face. She was wear-ing this camel-colored skirt, and I remember how she looked down and first saw the blood from Eddie not on me but on her skirt and how she screamed a little tight scream, like it had been wrong to scream under a porch, and asked me how I got all bloody, was I hurt.

"No," I told her.

"Did something happen to Guy?" she asked.

"It's Eddie," I whispered, and I was shaking all over. Even my voice was shaking like an old man's voice. And she pulled me by my arm into our house and saw Eddie right on the car-pet there and listened for breathing or a pulse. Then she let out this one cry like it was all she had left in her and picked up the phone and called 911. And she was trembling so much and cry-ing so hard that the lady had trouble understanding her, and she had to say it all again and again, maybe four times. And every time I heard her say it, it sounded different. "A child has been shot here, a child has been shot here," she kept repeating, and she never said it the same, and she never once mentioned me.

Then she phoned Frank at work and they whispered for a few seconds. I think she said something terrible had happened and that he should come home immediately. Then she propped the door a little open and sat down on the carpet next to Eddie and motioned for me to come to her, and I kind of folded into her lap and slept for what felt like a long time, but it must have been short because the record said that 911 came to our house four minutes and fifty-four seconds after her call.

That's how I killed Eddie and that's how everyone's lives changed forever.

15

I DIDN'T MEAN to kill Eddie.

Maybe I did mean to kill Eddie. He was always in my face and didn't seem to understand how to be fair about anything. And it made me so mad that he was pretending to shoot Guy and that he was blocking my door.

But that wouldn't make me mean to kill Eddie. I don't think most of the time that I meant to kill Eddie.

16

SINCE I KILLED Eddie I've read the story about Orion, who was a giant hunter and got placed in the stars by Diana after she killed him. I can locate Orion in the sky, and I think about him a lot. More though, I think about Eddie and my mom and me and how so many terrible things happen all the time.

I've watched a lot of news lately, and every day I see people dying in different ways. Sometimes 149 people go at once because some nut sets off a bomb. Or a divorce attorney gets mailed a nice Christmas package that explodes, and he loses both hands. Or a father and son get stuck in a blizzard while they're skiing, and only the son survives until morning. I think of him lying beside his father's body and wondering why he got to live.

That's what I think about all the time, why it was me who got to live and not Eddie. And I really can't say why. If you're real religious, no matter what religion, I guess you believe that everything has a purpose. But maybe things got mislaid that winter. Maybe it got so cold because someone (or something) wasn't watching. Maybe God was hibernating. Or maybe he was so busy somewhere else that no one was watching that afternoon.

I know that lots of times the doctor has asked me if I think it's my mother's fault and I always say the same thing, "I killed Eddie, not my mother." But it's true that if my mother was home, this wouldn't have happened. When my mother was home, Eddie and I would play video games and wrestle at the most. Mothers make the world safe for kids. Maybe they're the ones who watch everything. But I haven't had a dad for nine years, and my mother has to support us, and it was too cold for Aunt Sheila to take buses and el trains just to watch me and, besides, I was eleven.

In some countries, I've seen this on the news, kids my age make rugs all day or get recruited into the army and carry machine guns. So I don't think you can blame my mother at all.

Sometimes I think that you can kind of blame Frank for making a weapon so available to Eddie. I mean, why didn't he keep it in his trunk so no one could get their hands on it when he wasn't around? But it seems kind of creepy to blame Frank. After all, he lost his son, so who's going to tell him to be wiser in the future?

I miss Eddie more than I ever imagined I could. Sometimes when I lie in bed, I hear him talking to me, but I guess it's my voice that I hear because it's more like what I'd say. I pretend Eddie is telling me we both should have been more careful, like we're sharing the blame, but I know that's just me trying to feel better before I fall asleep. And I hope some day that Eddie says he forgives me when we have these midnight chats, but I don't see why he should. He misses his whole life and I still have mine, whatever it's worth.

Part Three

Frank

BECAUSE HIS FATHER was so mean—what else was there to call it?—he was perpetually recalled and perpetually hated. It came to the son as naturally as breath, an acrid morning taste, the thought of the small, compact man. He could picture his mother, beige as sand—hair, skin, dress—smoothing down her husband's swirled, nonconforming hair, and whispering tenderly into his ear, dead as stone. But he couldn't imagine his father, gone four years, mute and almost blind, rendered molelike by a series of strokes, or lying soft as grass in his grave.

Even now, approaching forty years old, commanding a vehicle that weighed nearly three tons, he was sullen, bitter, an angry child. His own gray hair had overrun the darker crop, crow's feet were apparent, and the skin beneath his chin sagged a little, perceptible more by touch than vision. His image grew more fragile, more contingent daily in his eye. It had never gained dignity nor its precursor, validity. It was the same abstraction in the series of photos, one of each decade, placed together like a lineup of crude selves in his mind. Equally throughout his life they'd contributed to one label. As his car drifted north on the interstate that would take him to his brother's dismal parcel of land in Wisconsin, he was a victim as much as ever, a perpetual boy: Frank Nova, who had already lost a father and now a son.

From reading the musculature of his father's sinewy cheeks, which tensed in frequent disapproval, Frank's eyes had taken on a permanent watchfulness. Like an animal Frank could survey the air that surrounded him and take refuge when it signaled imminent danger. Or, impersonal, more like a tree, he could stand stock-still and accept the blows his father visited upon him with a stoicism not usually associated with childhood.

Frank knew that he had used his ability to disengage while working as a paramedic. When suffering humanity presented itself to him, Frank Nova routinely and methodically pulled out overeager newborns, massaged impassive hearts, searched for pulses, stanched arteries spouting blood, shut gaping eyes and spread white sheets. Maybe his feeling of protective detachment, of outward rather than inward engagement, pulled the car north like metal attracted to a distant magnet. Truthfully, if he examined his feelings, he would just as soon be in a ditch, a piece of the mechanism, metal indistinct from tortured skin, blood, and bone.

But if his wife's version of heaven were true, if the forgiveness she had no time to dispense on Earth were bestowed there, if his daughter's simple view that "Eddie is with the angels" had meaning beyond the tacky cards he'd seen everywhere in stores, even roadside diners, maybe many years from now he'd approach its gates without a sneer of self-contempt.

Buzzing with decades-old rage, his mind filled with examples of his father's disapproval. He'd been no older than Eddie the year that his arm was so strong that he could strike out batters at will. He had the rare combination of a fastball and a

curve, too. Even good eyes got fooled by a ball that spun later-
ally, catching the air as it curved, at the last instant, directly
toward the plate. And pitching to small people was no mean
feat. Think of the trick Bill Veeck pulled having a midget bat
for his team. Had he ever told Eddie about Bill Veeck, he asked
the buzzing, warm air of the car?

That was the problem with Eddie gone. He couldn't tell him
the many things he had planned. Like how it feels to have sex
for the first time. How a woman's body, at least the few he had
known, could become more real than his own. Would Frank
have told his son that? Probably practical advice instead—to
wear condoms and be careful not to have a kid too soon. Too
many of Frank's high school buddies had gotten their lives all
messed up with that. Still in their late thirties, Donnys and
Craigs and Randys and Mortons were grandfathers now. Not
like it's ever time to have a kid if you think about it, but he
wouldn't have told Eddie that dismal fact.

He imagined that some day he would have explained to his
son about himself and Marilyn, so Eddie wouldn't think it was
his doing. The fact was, and he wished Eddie could have considered this truth a long time from now, that Frank had stayed
until Marilyn didn't want him anymore. Here he addressed
Eddie by name, as if his presence were distilled in the very air
of the car. He had been a father Eddie's entire life. What happened with Nancy had helped him last at it. He wouldn't think
of what more it had meant to him, this sweet wordless joining
in the dead of night, the electric touch of hands in curious
locations: garages and washrooms and fishing piers, under the
eyes of children, friends, and wives. All that, too, was behind a
padlocked door. The future no longer held Frank's normal life,
gone as a burnt page of a book, gone as animals that have

passed from the Earth. What had Frank thought calling Nancy to the station that night? More than anything, their last meeting was merely a diorama of something irretrievable.

Ruin was everywhere, impermanence certain, but Nancy had been a temporary barrier against his private chaos. She had been Frank's marriage insurance. With Nancy there had been no need to consider how bad it all was, how old, how mean, how exhausted it had become. As long as Frank had Nancy, Marilyn hadn't seemed to mind either. More than anything, Marilyn—"Your mom," he said as if to explain to Eddie, "wanted to be left alone." She needn't be reminded of what it meant to marry so young, or what her church would think if she simply admitted the truth—(and here he paused—some concepts are nearly unthinkable)—that Marilyn had stopped loving Frank a long time ago. What do popes know about love and how it can disappear like a wisp of smoke? The pope should try this highway into Wisconsin and see all the sex shops built as a monument to the failure of lasting arrangements.

Frank couldn't really say how it had happened, but he had an idea that when Carly was born, Marilyn realized that she could love someone better than Frank. Not that she hadn't loved Eddie—but Carly was special. Having a girl gave her an ally. More important, it gave her back to herself. She could make Carly into her understudy but leave out all the trouble, all the pain and compromises that life had dished out. That's what had united Frank and Marilyn in the beginning. They had homes they ached to leave. Fleeing them together formed a bond. Even when that bond had eased, Frank continued his project with Eddie, to create a version of himself that wouldn't flinch when a man lifted a hand in his direction. He was creating a new structure with big sunlit windows and a solid foundation.

On the last day of the regular season during that tenth memorable summer, Frank had gone to his baseball game alone. His parents weren't there to hear the announcement that he had been named to the all-star team. He remembered running home through the dusky light and thick air of late July in Chicago, running all the way up the back stairs of their red brick two-flat to tell his dad the good news. Husband and wife, back from a meeting of the church building committee, were seated at the mottled Formica kitchen table. His mother was holding a glass of lemonade. His father was drinking a Schlitz. Frank remembered the entire kitchen gleaming a warm, pale yellow, the color of movie cinematography when an intimate moment is looming. But the color of memories can be misleading. It can be inexact. It can commit fraud. What Frank now attaches to that yellow glow is deception.

Frank's parents looked vaguely at their son, whose excited shout filled the kitchen like a good cooking aroma. His mother offered her tolerant smile, the calm countenance she readied for bad news as well. Frank might just as well have said, "I got my bike stolen" or, later in life, "I knocked up the Devito girl." Only his dad's reply was apropos: "You'll ruin your arm before it's worth anything if you keep this up. You're just giving it away, Frank." Frank returned to this tableau ardently as the owner of a lost limb tries to recover the source of his pain.

Frank assumed that it was his dad's life in the Depression that made him assign value to everything. He had nothing as a boy, his family less, so nothing he had gained in life could be recognized as a gift or a boon. If it wasn't ruined, it was endangered. It was about to spoil. It needed to be hidden and maybe forgotten to maintain its perilous tangibility. He begrudged his children their presents at Christmas. "This is more than I got my whole life!" He berated his wife for the one trifle she had chosen aside from socks, slippers, and sensible underwear.

So even when Eddie was trouble, Frank vowed he would never act as angry as his dad, never make Eddie feel that even the air he breathed was being monitored for how it was wasted. Frank had wanted Eddie to inhale and exhale without pressure. At this thought he dabbed his eyes and blinked quickly at the road, which rose and fell in abrupt waves. Several cars whizzed by on his right, and he noticed how slowly he had been going in the passing lane, fifty and dropping. Sometimes Frank had been lax, it was true. He should have told Eddie to stop when he hadn't, but what could be so wrong about a little freedom, a little sunshine to walk through? If he had come down hard on Eddie now and then, the boy might have listened better, but Frank figured that he should learn to be the patient one, not a little boy who couldn't even sit still and whose first urge in life was to feel no consequences.

Frank began to address Eddie now, calling the invisible presence "you" and watching his lips in the rearview mirror. "Even when you tried my patience, I turned the other cheek. Like when you threw Danny's cap in the river and I had to wade in up to my waist."

And now he can't help but pause to think—and the tears well up—how his permissiveness helped Eddie take the bow next door. His panic rises and adrenaline pumps the gas pedal to eighty, eight-five, ninety, as he tries to do what?—flee himself? Maybe Nancy was right. The bow was the problem. He had caused the trouble by giving Eddie the bow, Eddie who would have never had even a damn army knife or a baseball cap if he had been Frank's father's son. Eddie couldn't have aimed it at the dog or at Danny if he'd had any fear. Are fear and good sense necessarily linked?

But Frank wasn't put on Earth to be a cop. "I never hit you, never lifted my hand once. That speaks for itself," he murmurs. His father had been so free with his hands that sometimes he boxed the wrong kid's ears. And if Ronnie or C. J. or Frank complained, he would smile this nasty little smile, how a weasel might bare its teeth, and say "It all evens out. Next time I'll get the wrong kid again, and then it'll be fair."

When Ronnie left for Viet Nam and wouldn't even visit after he returned home decorated and quietly celebrated in army circles, Frank had a sense of how they would all make out in life. They'd be nothing. That was it—the kinds of guys who are never comfortable with themselves, even when they're men and have people calling them *sir*. Dogs with their tails between their legs.

Frank had seen a picture of Ronnie's place once, a run-down farmhouse out in the woods. Ronnie who could fix anything and was gentle with everyone. He was the kind one in the family, no matter what his dad had done to alter that. Frank couldn't help but hear the high wounding voice of the old man as he looked at the photo of his son the hero's hideout in the woods. "Why's he hiding up there in a shack?" the old man cracked, never understanding his own part in Ronnie's retreat.

C. J., too, had his troubles. On the books, you'd think he was making out in life with his executive office and shares in the fiber-optics corporation. He had the fortune and the house and the boat and the custom cars. He had the drinking and the early heart bypass and no wife anymore just like Frank. She had left years ago with the kids. At first C. J. wanted his kids back, but finally he settled for the dog, who one day wandered off and turned up at the veterinarian's office. Maybe the dog had thought it was too damn embarrassing to be C. J.'s dog. Now C. J. was never at home because he had nothing to keep him there.

After Eddie died, Frank began having trouble sleeping. Nights on duty, he did a little better. But the house was always so quiet. Once it held no possibility of Eddie's noise, it was like sleeping in a morgue. Not that Frank could believe in ghosts— it's almost the next century—but there was something in the air that never let go.

Finally, he saw a doctor who gave him pills the size of Communion wafers and told him to take two at night. Then he slept like he was dead. He'd wake with the sickening knowledge that he had nothing, only to have Marilyn reinforce the feeling by acting as if he weren't there. She'd carved things up. Frank got Eddie and Marilyn got Carly. "With you gone, Eddie," Frank says quietly, almost prayerfully, "I lost my claim."

But realizing that and living that are two different things. You can go from room to room with the desperate energy of loss. Frank did nothing during the day, yet it exhausted him just to sit at the kitchen table. When Marilyn told him in no uncertain terms just to get the hell out, he felt secretly overjoyed, but as soon as he drove away, the illusion was gone.

He'd been emptied out, completely. He felt as if there had been a scalpel so delicate and a surgeon so skilled that he could carve the person out of its form and leave something else standing there that had his name but was missing every other measure of identity. He realized how it was to be his father, someone who felt nothing but anger at not feeling. That's when he decided that he needed to drive north.

The sense of Eddie still existing was so strong that sometimes, as now, he addressed him in the first person. He'd been doing that more lately. Maybe some trucker hauling steel beams saw a man moving his lips as he drove, but how odd would that be? People act like cars are bathrooms and living rooms these days, flossing their gums, talking on phones, reading a magazine or two as they peer over the steering wheel. Nothing is so odd about a man speaking to no one in the car, about lips moving, maybe to music or maybe in prayer. We own what we miss as much as we own anything, Frank thinks, as he slows to exit the interstate. He needs a beer and a few shots and maybe the kid in back, concealed under blankets, hands and feet bound, mouth taped shut, is feeling hungry by now.

Every boy's walk, rumpled jeans, bony shoulder blades, head of hair, easy smile, reminded Frank of what he had lost. Kids in television shows resembled his son. There was a radio commercial for an amusement park whose child actor had Eddie's springy laugh. Frank's dreams filled with scenes of his son climbing out of windows, dangling perilously from rooftops, holding on to a breaking beam and asking to be saved. Meanwhile, Frank, repairer of bodies, healer of wounds, could only watch in one corner of the room, inert as the dream chair he occupied.

Frank walked numbly through the world wondering how such a thin, erratic line could separate life and death. His own existence had come to contain neither figure nor ground, no reassuring contrasts worth noting. Eddie was more alive in Frank's life than he was in his own. He was empty of what he needed even to play at living. That's why he had stopped seeing Carly, his eager second child, all ballet poses and ready smiles. She didn't speak of Eddie, but what could Frank guess of how a little girl might feel absence even as she moved through the spaces her body inhabited?

Frank no longer had the ability to give consolation or to be consoled. That's why the numerous attempts of friends from work to invite him into their homes had failed. That's why his night with Nancy, a stupid idea to begin, had progressed from dread to rage to a simple desire for his own swift annihilation. He felt nothing at all, even as he rocked upon her sweet accepting body, the one he had needed as dearly as air.

When he'd discovered Danny in the park, his presence seemed an error, an alien color in Frank's wintry palette. At first Frank had no thought of taking Danny anywhere. More than anything, he wanted to erase him, as one would any gross inconsistency. But even as he thought of escaping from the huge contradiction of Danny's life before his eyes, he craved more contact. He wanted to maybe embrace the boy, maybe to slap him, and then measure what life remained in him. Like a seismometer, his reaction to Danny might reveal vibrations hidden to his own eye and ear.

It was one of those rare days of April in Chicago, when mottled islands of leftover ice slowly melt and a few brave buds develop on trees. There would probably be three more frosts before green things were really safe. Frank remembered once, having started a garden too soon, he'd needed to cover everything in plastic overnight. Still, buds had frozen on vines and branches, and May had arrived without the usual fanfare.

"Danny," he said quietly, tentatively, when he was close enough to touch the boy. He wondered if Danny would recognize what was left of him.

"Hi, Mr. Nova," Danny said with slight hesitation. It was the same voice Frank remembered from a life now centuries removed from this day. His face looked pinched and tense, an expression of pain that mirrored Frank's. There was an indelible sadness about Danny's olive-drab eyes despite the lovely weather and his eager posture on the swing that barely stirred in the breeze. "I just got home two days ago," he said flatly.

"I know." Frank felt suddenly sweaty, feverish in the mild sun. His body was ready to desert his suddenly curious mind.

"I was there a long time," Danny said softly. It almost sounded like he was giving Frank a cue, permission to say something angry or unkind.

And just as Frank felt pity surge and flood him with unnamed relief, just as he was about to reassure Danny that it was really no one's fault, not his, not Eddie's, not Danny's, not Nancy's, not Marilyn's, not even Frank's father's, just as he thought of clutching the boy and pressing him close, cleansed in welcome forgiveness, he felt a different urge.

He needed Danny. He didn't understand for what purpose. He just knew that he needed him as much as he had needed anyone ever. If Frank was going to live through this, if he was ever going to get back the significance to life that Eddie's death had extinguished, Danny had something to do with it. As he drove north, as he dismissed his father from his thoughts, as he imagined himself arriving unannounced on Ronnie's land, Frank knew that Danny was his armor and his necessary resilience.

It was that simple, how Danny had ended up with Frank. Frank quietly told him that his mother wanted him fetched from the park. And Frank didn't change his story until they were well out of Chicago. Danny found himself on some nameless mile of highway joining Illinois to its northernmost border. He felt desperate to tell his mother that it wasn't his fault that he couldn't get a haircut and new jeans later that afternoon. What would she think when he didn't return, and the empty park was unable to disclose his whereabouts? She would think that he couldn't be trusted, that he really was crazy to flee the home whose welcome had caused him to weep quiet tears two nights earlier.

Because Nancy had suffered enough lately, it was impossible for Danny to separate the guilt he felt for her suffering from his current sense of being in danger. Both feelings welled up in his throat simultaneously, making it hard for him even to form sounds though he had spoken to Frank Nova thousands of times. He had said more to Frank than to any other man in his life, but when he finally found the words, "Where are we going?" they sounded small and hollow and ready to evaporate on his tongue.

Instead of answering, Frank simply speeded up. It seemed as though Danny's every query resulted in a new blast on the accelerator. Finally, Danny figured it was safer to be quiet than to goad someone so desperate that his driving was impaired. Frank's agitated silence stoked Danny's fears, causing his whole body to tremble. He couldn't sit still to save his life. His legs quivered, his hands jiggled in his lap, and even his head seemed to be inwardly buzzing. He needed to get out, but the car was continuing to lurch ahead in abrupt bursts of speed followed by momentary slackening.

After he softly whimpered "Frank" about a dozen times to no result, Danny decided on a plan. If he could make Frank feel a little scared, maybe he could get a response out of him. Quietly Danny's hand fumbled for the door handle. Then a hurried gesture opened it to a wedge the size that someone might need to get rid of a piece of chewed gum. Danny immediately felt Frank's fingers wrapping hard around the back of his neck. His long-awaited voice finally formed words, a soft muttering sound, which Danny couldn't reconcile with such a blunt message: "You're coming with me."

"Does my mom want that?" Danny whispered, voice cracked with the awareness that this drive had nothing to do with her plans.

Frank pulled over, but even as he left the road, his hand remained fastened on Danny's neck. It made the boy wonder how someone could have so much physical control that one hand could hold on to a person and the other steer a car off the road. But when he thought more about it, he decided maybe people seem most in control when they're afraid or angry or simply broken. That's something he had learned in the hospital, that not even adults know what they feel half the time. It didn't need to make sense that Frank was stealing Danny from a park in daylight and taking him who knows where.

Danny wasn't convinced that Frank would harm him. He couldn't imagine a grown man, a father, seeking revenge until Frank's hand exerted ominous pressure and the car rolled onto the shoulder of the road. Then, unwinding the fingers from Danny's neck, Frank seized Danny's arm and wrenched it behind his back in the same flowing gesture. Pulling the boy toward him as he stepped out of the driver's side, they walked awkwardly toward the trunk. After taking something from it which Danny couldn't see, he once again seized Danny's neck and forced him into the backseat with an abruptness that betrayed no concern for Danny's head, which soundly struck the car door frame. A short whimper of pain as Frank shoved him across the backseat and, breathless now, used hands and mouth to pull off tape and wrap up Danny's wrists and ankles and close his mouth and lay him there. Trembling, Danny found himself prone on the backseat, head throbbing.

When he continued to whimper through the tape, Frank got out of the car again. He came back with a dirty beige tablecloth that Danny recognized from picnics taken when life was still an ordinary routine. It was the same they'd used to cover an old green metal table on their fishing trip to the Kankakee River. Draping him in it now, Frank began to speak. "You'll just have to lie still and be quiet, Danny." Frank managed an even tone of voice that seemed full of sense. Later, when Danny recalled these words, he was almost certain that Frank had called him Eddie.

Danny

THE MAN WHO played Superman cries every morning when he wakes up and finds himself still paralyzed, but being a prisoner wasn't that bad, Danny told himself when he opened his eyes. Frank's brother Ronnie didn't have things like a phone or regular mail pickup, but Danny could still use his arms and legs and all the muscles he had to do something about his situation. He thought of escaping every day.

He hadn't seen or heard from another person since he and Frank arrived. Mostly he just sat around thinking that things couldn't go on like this forever. By September when school started he'd be right back on the third floor with Mrs. Dubois, who was supposed to be pretty nice. And maybe he'd even be home by the all-star break. Danny didn't understand how Ronnie could live all alone without a TV.

By now Danny was sure that his mom had reported him lost or stolen and that people were out looking. It would be hard for them to ignore that Frank was missing, too. When Danny used to talk with Riley about detectives, he'd heard a story about a man named Brandy who Riley had known in Ireland a long time ago. Once Brandy looked for a stolen thoroughbred horse for two years before he found it—all that time for a horse! And when he found it the bad guys had turned it another color.

Danny knew that detectives don't just work on a case for a weekend like it seems on television. Sometimes it takes them years to solve one, only Danny's case won't take so long once they figured out it was Frank who has taken him. Sooner or later, a detective was going to drive up the road and find him just like that. Danny imagined how he'd wake up to see smiling strangers staring down at him like he was a chunk of gold. They'd probably have a photograph that they'd hold up to his face to make a comparison. Danny tuned his ear for the sound of car wheels on the gravel. Sometimes he imagined a megaphone voice saying, "Danny, come out. And you, Nova, come out too, only with your hands up." Meanwhile, there was a pretty nice dog, a curly mutt named Royal, who let Danny throw its old rag toy around all day and never got sick of chasing it.

Sometimes when Danny had bad dreams, he would wake up shaking, eyes wide open all night while he wondered whether Frank and his brother weren't crazy. Who but crazy people would have taken a boy? There were laws in the United States. Ronnie couldn't think that just because he lived in the woods and didn't have a single friend those laws didn't apply anymore.

At night Danny's door was locked from the outside. The room, which had no window, was connected to the kitchen. Danny could only escape if they let him out, which never happened at night. If he had to pee, there was a bottle to use.

Danny thought Ronnie looked like someone had taken Frank and stretched him. But Ronnie was quieter than his brother. Usually when he talked, it was about some momentary business. He'd ask Danny if he wanted tomato soup or just some bread and butter for lunch.

Ronnie had some nice collections that Danny supposed he'd

started as a boy. One was a can full of matches from places he used to go. He didn't have anything new in the can. Some of the matches were real funny, like extra long ones with a drawing of a hot dog from some place called Denny's Foot Longs and pink ones with the silhouette of a lady's shoe from a place called Estelles. But Danny couldn't get Ronnie to say a thing about the matches.

Conversations went like this:

"Those are your matches?"

"Yeah."

"Why did you want to collect matches?"

"I went places and got them."

"Why don't you go anywhere now?"

"Just don't."

And then Ronnie would squeeze up his face and almost close his eyes like he was squinting at something far away in his memory. Danny would know that Ronnie was finished talking for the rest of the day.

Ronnie's other collection was dirt. He had jars from every state he'd ever visited, fourteen, and some from Viet Nam. For someone who didn't like to go anywhere, Ronnie sure had peculiar hobbies.

Frank was away most mornings. Danny wasn't sure where he went. He'd be out of the house real early, before anyone was up, and later, usually around lunchtime, he'd come back just as abruptly. Once he brought a couple of fish on a string that looked like he'd caught them, and Ronnie fried them for supper. Once he got a new battery for Ronnie's old pickup, which wouldn't start even after all the time they spent on it that afternoon. Another day he'd brought Danny a package of birthday balloons when it wasn't even his birthday.

When Frank was away, Ronnie was supposed to watch

Danny, but when he had work to do around the place, he'd leave Danny sitting in the front room bored out of his mind. Danny could hear him hammering all morning or sawing wood or sometimes snoring back in bed like there was just no reason to stay awake. Before Ronnie took his naps, he'd lock Danny back in his room and give him a lot of old magazines from the seventies. They were all about disco dancing and Nixon. Danny imagined that Ronnie must have stopped reading around 1974.

Every day Danny would wake up about the same time and get dressed and wait. Frank had bought him underwear, socks, and a few new shirts. Danny guessed that Frank planned on staying for a while. Every day Danny tried to wear something different because it would be bad to just stay in bed and not care how you looked. If he started that with the way things were, he might just sleep forever.

It was a good thing that the weather was getting better because a boy could only look at dirt and matches so long before going nuts. Now Danny could take the dog outside and play all over the place. They would make big loops in the gravel in front. Danny would press real hard in the driveway, leaving a message for anyone to see.

Sometimes when he walked down the road a little with Royal following him, everything felt fine. It almost seemed that life was normal. Ronnie didn't seem to mind if he strayed a little. Danny would throw an old bitten tennis ball as high as he could into the sky and Royal would wait for it to drop. The dog usually caught it on the second bounce.

Danny found all kinds of junk on Ronnie's property, including the shell of an old stripped-down car. Danny would sit in this dirty yellow Plymouth Fury and talk out loud to his mother. He told her that he was doing okay. He named exactly the place he was, so maybe she could somehow find him. He wrote her name on the windows so that when the light was just right, anyone could see "Nancy Nancy Nancy" sprawling all over the place. Danny thought of this as his work, leaving a series of clues.

He could see his mother's face and hear her voice easily in his head. He could picture dead people in his mind or people he hardly ever saw, like his real father. Lots of times he saw Eddie. Mostly he looked alive but sometimes he was dead. When Eddie was alive, Danny would always see him smiling. Danny would think how terrible it was that Eddie would never get older. Eddie would never get to know if there was life on Mars or who would be president in 2010. Eddie didn't look bad dead. His face wasn't angry, but Danny thought it should be. He'd lost everything, and Danny was still looking at the sky and sneezing from the sunshine and eating bread and sometimes laughing at a joke he remembered. Thinking that always made him cry, especially the part about the sky.

At the hospital around his birthday Danny couldn't stop seeing Eddie for a while. That's why he was sawing on his wrist that day. He noticed that when he hurt himself, he could stop thinking. Sometimes he pinched himself real hard or bit his cheek until it would start bleeding. Now when he wanted to feel better, Danny would picture his mom, who always looked like she'd just come home from work and was ready to make him dinner. He used to imagine her a lot in the hospital, too, but sometimes it didn't help. He wished he could send his mom letters like he did when he was away the last time. With Frank gone the other day, he'd written her a long letter and asked Ronnie to mail it. Ronnie looked worried when he took it out of Danny's hand.

Once when Frank was away and it was real quiet around

lunchtime, Danny asked Ronnie if he knew about Eddie. Ronnie stared at him like he was sad Danny had asked.

"Did you know Eddie?" he asked again.

"Sure I did," Ronnie said, but then he walked outside to sweep the porch with the dirty old broom he used, and it didn't look like he wanted to talk much to Danny again. Ronnie had the cleanest porch around from all the times he walked out there not to talk. Sometimes Danny would sweep his porch, too. Danny thought it was like a disease you caught at Ronnie's, this interest in not talking.

Tonight was going to be special because someone named LuAnn was coming to dinner. She was someone Ronnie had known for a long time, and Frank seemed happy she'd been invited. Maybe Frank was happy that Ronnie knew someone, but if Danny were Frank, he'd worry that Ronnie was having someone to dinner. Frank didn't seem worried about much at all. Danny wondered if when you're crazy you just stop worrying. He knew he'd be worried every second if he'd taken someone else's kid and not told anyone. He'd worry all day and even in his sleep.

Frank had gone to town for groceries and planned on making chili for Ronnie's guest. Danny imagined that before Frank came, Ronnie must have walked into town now and then, so it couldn't be that far. Danny hoped Frank would buy some lettuce and Paul Newman dressing and maybe a frozen cake to serve because just chili in a bowl isn't very nice for a dinner guest. Sometimes when Danny's mom made chili, she'd serve pieces of cheese in it or bake cornbread on the side, but she'd never make it for company. His Aunt Sheila used to make chili with raisins and cashews in it, but nobody really liked it, and she finally stopped.

About an hour before LuAnn was supposed to arrive for dinner, Frank said, "Time to eat." Danny sat at the kitchen table, which was really an old picnic table with a bench for one side and two chairs for the other. In front of Danny's usual seat was a big bowl of chili and a glass of milk that had a chili hand-print on it from how much Frank was rushing. He told Danny to eat fast because LuAnn would be coming soon.

As Danny ate as fast as he could, he was beginning to guess that Frank had something in mind. "How long am I supposed to stay with you here?" he asked.

"As long as I need you," Frank shrugged.

"What exactly do you need me for?" Instead of answering, Frank motioned for Danny to follow him. He walked out the front door and around the side of Ronnie's house. Danny followed him to a locked door the color of green Easter mints, which was both part of the house and part of the ground. A person would never have a door like that in Chicago.

Because it was almost May, the days were getting longer and at seven at night, it wasn't quite dark. Still, Danny could see the moon and a few clouds lapping over it. He took a deep breath and tried not to show he was afraid, but he felt more afraid than he'd been since Frank taped him all up and covered him with a tablecloth in the car.

"Where am I going?" he asked Frank as they stood in front of the mysterious door.

"In there," Frank explained, as he squatted to open the lock. Danny decided he needed to do something. Being in the house was bad enough. He wasn't going to let himself be locked in the basement for the night. It was probably dark and smelly in there. Danny couldn't imagine himself underground while three people at a table were pretending there was nothing wrong in the world. They'd get all the light they wanted and all the food, and they'd talk about normal things like planting beans or reading library books. Just thinking about it made Danny's ankles feel nauseated, like he needed to run forever.

He took off right then, faster than he thought he could, racing toward the front and out of the yard. Before Frank had straightened up from bending over and fussing with the lock, Danny was a few hundred yards into the woods down the road. He was probably too far away for Frank to hear his strained breathing, but he knew that Frank would be looking for him. He twisted himself up behind a broken old fence and some thick trees that smelled like gumdrops and tried to control his fear. He could always sleep in the Plymouth. There was a passenger door that no one could see open from any angle of the house. He knew it was comfortable in there. Danny hated to think about sleeping outside in the woods and waking up all achy, covered with dew and snails. That once happened to him when he slept in his yard in a little tent his mother had bought.

Danny could imagine two possible plans. He could roam around until he found a road that took him to someone's house. Then he'd ask to be let in. Probably there were farmers all over the place, a family with children somewhere nearby who'd be happy to help him out. They'd even end up heroes if they let Danny call his mother, who'd call the police. Then he wouldn't have to wait for Frank not to need him anymore, whatever that meant anyway.

Maybe Danny should do something riskier. He could come right back while Frank and Ronnie and LuAnn were eating dinner. Then he'd tell his whole story right in front of her. But Ronnie and Frank might just say Danny was nuts, or maybe if LuAnn was friends with Ronnie, she'd be crazy too and not even believe him. Or Frank might pretend that Danny was his son with too lively an imagination. How would LuAnn know who was telling the truth? It could even turn out worse. Frank could simply tell LuAnn that Danny had killed Eddie. No one would ever want to listen to Danny again, no matter what. And maybe when LuAnn heard what he'd done, she'd say that Danny deserved to be someone's prisoner.

That was the last thought he had before Frank was with him again. The sky was black by now and clouds were a stringy, clotted gray. Danny was shivering because it had gotten a lot colder, so it must have been hours later. Danny remembered how sometimes when you sleep, you wake up because someone is staring at you. That was how it happened. Danny must have felt Frank kneeling right across from him and opened his eyes.

"Okay," Frank said quietly.

Danny was blinking, trying to adjust to the darkness and wondering what exactly was okay.

"Ronnie's gone to LuAnn's for the night."

"Is she his girlfriend?"

"Sort of."

"Did she know Eddie?"

"No. Now come back to the house," Frank said in a peaceful way. "It's too cold to spend the night outside."

They walked back in silence. Frank kept his arm firmly around Danny's neck.

The moon was all boxed in by the gritty clouds. Danny gave it a last quick look before stepping into the house just in front of Frank. He thought how the same moon was everywhere, over half of the world, how his mother might be seeing it right now, too.

The front door groaned shut, but as Danny walked toward his room, he heard Frank telling him to sit down.

"How long do I have to stay here?" he asked as soon as he seated himself across from Frank.

"Till you're sleepy."

"No, I mean *here*."

"I don't know, Danny."

"Do you think a lot about how it could be different?"

"I think about that all the time." Frank paused. "I think about him . . . like he's still here."

"Me, too."

Danny watched Frank. He almost wished that Frank would want Danny to hug him, but that seemed too much to imagine. Frank looked all private and huddled into himself like he was becoming a statue. That's what the doctor said would happen to Danny if he didn't talk more about himself and Eddie. He might just turn into a stone.

"Frank," Danny said very cautiously. "Do you want to talk more?"

The sounds of the room answered: boards creaking, wind slapping the door, the roof rattling like maybe squirrels were chasing each other in great mindless circles.

That's all he heard as he finally walked off to his room and crawled into bed, but a few minutes later, Frank's voice breathed in his doorway.

"Sleep tight," he said before he locked Danny in. Danny imagined how much Frank was wishing it was Eddie in the bed.

When Ronnie didn't come back the next day, it got quieter and quieter. Frank showed up in the same clothes to give Danny chili for breakfast and lunch and canned peaches and old bread for dinner. He toasted it first and left a tub of imitation butter out, but he didn't talk to Danny all day. Danny watched him read and reread an old *National Geographic,* one Danny had looked at before. It had pictures of some island where the monkeys were smaller than anywhere else on earth and an article about coal with lots of drawings of layers of dirt and rocks with dinosaur fossils stuck in them. Danny started to wonder if Frank was worried about where Ronnie was or whether he was just depressed that he couldn't go anywhere with Ronnie gone.

Before Ronnie had disappeared, Frank was able to enjoy some time away. Danny guessed that he used to spend some of it in a bar because his face looked red and blotchy when he'd come back and sometimes he'd talk way too loud or just fall asleep in a chair. His voice had a way of rising in each sentence like a wave. It seemed sad to Danny that bars were open so early for some people to drink gin and beer for breakfast.

Once his mother's college friend, Ethelbert, a black guy who had once been a pretty good poet, came to visit. He was a nice man, but after Danny's mom knew him, he had had a hard life. He'd even been in jail for stealing something at a gas station. Maybe Ethelbert had learned to like beer so much when he missed it in jail. Now he would leave beer in a paper bag outside on the window sill and have it ready to drink in the morning. Maybe he thought Danny's mom would be mad if he kept it in her refrigerator, which might have actually been better because beer can freeze outside in a cold climate. His mom had explained that Ethelbert needed some time to get back on his feet.

A few years after his visit, his mom told Danny that Ethelbert was dead. Danny remembered the toys he'd given Ethelbert to take home to his children, whom he seemed to really love. It was hard for Danny to understand something she explained later, that Ethelbert hadn't seen his kids almost since they were born. That made him more like Danny's father, but he still seemed a whole lot nicer. Danny's real father didn't have problems like Ethelbert, but he still hadn't wanted to know Danny very well. When Danny heard Ethelbert was dead, he just hoped that he'd gotten to know his kids first.

Now Danny was with Frank, who was no longer bathing and was growing a beard and was drinking a lot of something clear in a glass. Danny didn't think you would drink rum straight, so the glass must be gin or vodka. His Aunt Sheila liked to drink things with rum but there had to be juice and paper umbrellas.

By the second day, Danny thought Frank might really go insane. He spent most of his time pacing in front of the window and looking down the lane for Ronnie like guys in westerns look for gunmen holed up in the woods. Sometimes Danny looked, too, but it seemed to bother Frank when Danny stood too near him. He'd move to the other side of the room and eye Danny sideways like strangers do waiting for a bus.

"Maybe he married her," Danny said, but Frank didn't seem to notice.

Danny started fixing himself food whenever he needed to eat. There wasn't much, so mainly he had crackers and peanut butter and sardines when he finally figured out how to open the cans that have little keys and a thin line of tin like a zipper.

Danny didn't think Frank ever ate. It was like he wasn't human anymore. He would stay in the window and walk to the kitchen now and then to pour more stuff and then, really early, before the sun was down, he'd say "Time for bed." Once Danny's mom used a baby-sitter named Carmen who just wanted to have boys over. She'd make Danny go to bed at six-thirty. When he finally told his mom, she fired her.

Danny decided that staying out of Frank's way was a good idea when Frank tripped over a little kid's chair Ronnie had in the front room. Frank got so mad at the chair that he broke it to pieces and threw it out the door. If Ronnie had been around, he finally would have had something real to sweep.

Frank

ON THE THIRD morning of Ronnie's absence, Frank woke up and made the kind of bargain that superstitious people are prone to draw out of fear. If the sun over Ronnie's birch tree sat low on the leftmost branch, he'd give Danny back. When that wasn't the solar inclination, he added a proviso: if Ronnie's dog barked before Danny said his first word of the day, he'd return Danny right then. But he couldn't give Danny up any better than he could have revived Eddie once an arrow had stopped his heart. He and Danny were united for as long as Frank imagined continuing on earth.

He remembered his father having predicted his own death before the snow melted one bitter March. For once he had kept his word. That April, while crocuses nosed up through the ground, his father stood up from dinner with his wife, collapsed next to the kitchen chair, and never regained consciousness. Frank remembered his astonishment that it could be possible when Marilyn told him the news. He felt as if a siege had lifted and that he had miraculously survived despite dangerous service in the trenches. Given back his life, he responded dumbly to people's offerings of condolence.

It was only with his father gone that he could have found Nancy and lived in what he now viewed to have been an era of freedom. On many occasions Frank caught himself grinning or whistling, as if some personally involved God had awarded him a new destiny. Only then did he understand what it meant that Christ had been merciful to man. Being an adulterer had made him devout. He went to church to offer thanks. He lit candles and wadded dollars into the collection plate and sang hymns so avidly that Marilyn sometimes stared. As he pictured Nancy, small and eager for him under her paisley futon sheets, he took the Communion wafer and thanked God for the new life he'd been delivered.

While staying at his brother's, Frank thought of Nancy often, but his mind entertained many subjects. Really, he had never been so occupied as he had begun to feel here. Ronnie had nothing on hand to pass the time, not even a radio that worked, and Frank couldn't just go off and listen to music or news in his car, leaving the boy alone. The emptiness of the hours gave him a power of reflection he had never experienced before. He arranged all those still living as spokes on his wheel of loss. There was Marilyn and Carly, Nancy and Danny, himself and his brother, who appeared to have abandoned the mission.

Frank's retreat with Danny hadn't seemed to exist within boundaries until LuAnn had shown up. Time, which was how children grew to be men as birthdays passed like so much confetti, was no longer a factor. Probably LuAnn was keeping Ronnie in town with the kind of promises that a brother couldn't make. She was promising to keep Ronnie warm, Frank's poor dumb brother who still believed in consolation after all his years of hiding out. Ronnie was no different than Frank had been loving Nancy, bruised but not broken, ready to believe that someone—though the particular example of LuAnn was difficult to imagine under bright light—could change his life.

Frank was happy that Ronnie, who was a little "off," pretty sure that his brother with the cockeyed smile and uncurious eyes hadn't minded having the two of them in the house. Not many people would have adjusted as well to Frank and the child, but Ronnie wasn't like too many people. Until Frank came, he mostly sat around drunk for months at a time, he had reported to Frank. Since the VA told him he should have stopped drinking yesterday, he'd made an effort, but being alone and not drunk had only made him more lonesome.

About two years earlier, he'd met LuAnn. She was a VA nurse, and Ronnie had been her patient. Damned if he wasn't in the hospital laid up with a massive infection in his leg, a yellow runny mess that LuAnn had to clean with tweezers and gauze and salves. Damned if they hadn't fallen in love under those circumstances just like that. Ronnie didn't call it falling in love when he'd told Frank the story. He had just said that they'd taken a liking to each other. They were both pretty much alone, Ronnie had explained, so it fit the bill to have someone to talk to now and then. LuAnn had lived with her mother who'd died the winter before last, and Ronnie, well, he'd been alone as long as Frank could remember.

As Frank had anticipated, LuAnn wasn't much to look at, big and messy for a nurse, with apricot-colored hair that went every which way and a nose perpetually running. Mostly the nurses Frank had known at ERs were neat, compact things. LuAnn's arms were saggy with dimpled flesh. She wore no makeup and dressed exactly as Frank's mother did when she went to church on Palm Sunday in her best flowered blouse, polyester slacks, and sensible shoes.

But what did Ronnie need? Frank noticed how her head turned to Ronnie's voice. During the dinner, Frank felt envious for that kind of intimacy, the way something as simple as passing the butter or offering the salt and pepper could become an act of love. LuAnn was beautiful to Ronnie because she loved him; Frank or any fool could understand that. And within the dim blundering pain that filled Frank daily, a stab of wanting Nancy filtered through the blur of losing Eddie. He wanted them both, Eddie and Nancy, but Nancy alive was as impossible to recover as Eddie.

Frank wanted to tell his brother that he understood his loneliness, why he'd leave Frank and Danny for LuAnn, but each word was burdened with so much weight that even his thoughts felt heavy and discrete, like barges loaded with coal or toxic chemicals. He couldn't drift them toward the light of conversation. What could be said about forfeiting everything? Since Eddie had died he'd become a virtuoso of loss. He had examined every nuance of the word and begun to classify it in his leaden brain. There was the aloneness that he felt with people and they with him. There was Marilyn, who'd played dead whenever he approached her under the sheets. With Eddie gone, their isolation spread out like fog over other parts of their lives. They no longer looked at each other. If they had gained access to each other's eyes, their mutual presence would have confirmed something too awful to admit, even now, about life: look where it's led us. So without a glance, they had gotten through the funeral.

He could be close to no one now. There wasn't a way to hold Nancy or to touch her tiny, bell-shaped breasts. He couldn't take a pink nipple between his lips and suck without Eddie's face bobbing up like a buoy in night water. He couldn't even say her name and bring her image forth without the grief that finally shut him up again.

Having Danny around didn't ease the pain. It just froze it in position, like fixative over a slide of human hair. Frank probed every aspect of his suffering, and like a philosopher or mystic, chose to let it fill him with emotion rather than information. He forced himself out of the habit of response. He denied himself access to the ready reactions of the paramedic. Now he was more like the man, semiconscious and stumbling in the moonlight at the curb, who's been flung from his car driving home from work one night. He unlearned readiness. He refused to listen to his own body or mind as it indicated necessity. The sounds that told him if a person had enough blood in him to get from the red-stained street to an ER gurney became muted. He was dumb before the fact of his own devastation. Where had listening gotten him? When his child died right next door, almost in earshot, Frank hadn't been there. Nothing could change that.

Frank imagined that Danny was scared, but he had no intention of harming him. What good would that do, perverse revenge for something accidental, for using the weapon that he had taught the boy how to fire? No one could understand the purpose of Frank's retreat, to explore what it means to lose everything or why he needed to use Danny as the petri dish for his experiment.

The world wants action. It wants news to be news. Silence isn't news, so the world won't allow such a mute venture. Frank realized this even more acutely as he saw faces appear in the woods. Ronnie had done what a sane person would do, made a phone call. It was no act of betrayal. As isolated as Ronnie was, as sequestered, he was part of a world where life still made sense, action connected to action and yielded a result, love could be asked for and received, and fathers died before their sons.

Now that the police knew where Danny had gone, Nancy

would be located and called. She would be speeding toward Frank in a detective's black sedan. She would be licking her anxious lips and making nervous circles in her light-brown hair. She would be pained and sick with fear about her boy. But she would get Danny back. Unlike Frank, she had a future. And because of this difference, she would curse Frank or wish him dead for his futurelessness, for his despair. Maybe she would be able to get over this with Danny at her side. It was only when Frank thought about Nancy regaining her life that he ever considered harming Danny, not for taking Eddie away from this world but for still having Nancy with him in it.

Meanwhile, Frank knew that he would have to make plans. The men hidden in the trees weren't about to walk up to the door and knock politely. They anticipated more than a conversation with the lunatic in the woods. Based on the assumption that Frank was desperate and maybe mad, their tactics had to involve stealth and darkness.

In moments of lucidity, Frank agreed with their view of what holding Danny signified. People were probably calling it a hostage situation, so Frank adopted the vocabulary. What he hoped to do with his hostage when the moment was right— maybe even this night when a new group of watchers took the place of the original men—was take the boy to the car and drive far away, drive somewhere where no one could find them. Then, in an isolated place he imagined as a barren woods despite it being May, he would sit quietly at a table across from the boy. In his vision of this, the trees looked barely real, more like stage props. He also wondered why the table would suddenly be present in such a clearing. The goal of his dream of escape was a fuller opportunity to nurse his pain. Maybe years from now—if the authorities could be patient and he were allowed his silence—he'd have emptied himself of it. Maybe years from now, if he were allowed, he'd be fit for some kind of a life.

That was as close to hope as Frank ventured, but he doubted the men outside would understand. He could see them holding walkie-talkies and maybe rifles and looking in the direction of the house. Unaware of what essential ceremony required the captive boy, the police were ready to remove him. Not one of them, not even Ronnie if he were among them, could appreciate what it had come to mean to be Frank Nova. Frank suddenly had the whimsical thought that only Danny could possibly appreciate what it meant to be Frank Nova.

Looking out from the surrounded house, he determined that movement would soon be called for, but panic didn't seize him because sometimes miracles can happen just as accidents. Sometimes children get shot and are gone, and sometimes people sneak through the dark and get exactly where they're going and find themselves safe in the process. He thought of how fish move underwater, slow and unerring as their instincts prescribe. He and the boy would go down to the basement, break through to the root cellar, and get out of the house. They would dig through the half-frozen earth and come out into night and take off in the car. It was the first time Frank felt his practical wits returning since Eddie had been taken.

And for a minute he smiled toward Danny, who sat in a cold corner clutching his knees inside his circled arms, Danny who was afraid to look at Frank. What he must think of me, Frank remarked to himself, which led to something approaching a laugh forming near his lips before it burst inside the tense oval of his mouth.

Nancy

THE POLICE HAVE told Nancy that they'll find Danny later that day. They're that close. It's strange how having Riley Flowers along makes her so hopeful. She doesn't know what Riley has accomplished in his life, but Nancy does know that he's at her side, talking as they drive. He sees an old elm tree, which reminds him of a tree in their neighborhood, the last of its kind after Dutch elm disease ravaged its neighbors. He sees a house that reminds him of a friend's stone cottage in a town near Dublin that has a pub with four fireplaces and fieldstone chimneys and a satellite dish. He sees cows grazing, which remind him of his father's herd of Jerseys, how he'd milk them every night, how one long-legged specimen named Josephine seemed happier to see him than the rest. He says she mooed a special way when he arrived every night with the milk pail. What will he be reminded of when he sees her boy?

Nancy imagines what she'll do when she first sees Danny. She'll take him in her arms and smother him with hugs. That's what any mother would do. This ordeal has made her think of how people are all alike—even Frank for what he's done is like most people stricken with grief. What he has done with Danny, she has to keep telling herself, makes perfect sense if you're Frank.

When she pictures seeing Danny again, it's always a silent movie. No words exist to say to Danny what she's felt since Frank took him two and a half weeks ago. There's silence inside her, deep as any well, and when she imagines speaking, it grows. People are so poorly prepared for what they feel that what they come to understand can never really get spoken.

Sometimes she thinks that every story has its own language except for a few. Nancy has seen photos of people in Cambodia awaiting execution by the Khmer Rouge. There are no words for the story of how a child reaches her hands, the only part of her caught in the photo, for her mother. Words are about rescue, signaling for help. There is nothing she can say to Danny since she couldn't save him either time he needed saving.

She's read that animals who live in packs designate some of their kind to be watchmen for the group. They are the most nervous and most intelligent. All those years of having Danny alone, Nancy trained herself to seem calm. She talked herself out of knowing what she should have known to have given Danny the life everyone wants, the anonymous life. "And she gave him a life that no one remembers" should be the closing of fairy tales.

She remembers telling her mother that typical teenage line when she was seventeen and very angry. She didn't ask to be born, she shouted about something no more serious than a bad haircut. But a deeper pain cannot be spoken—she knows that to be true. If you can talk yourself into something or out of it, you're not in trouble yet.

Riley would understand this if she told him, but she's been thinking to herself for so long that when Nancy turns to tell him any part of this, she sees he's fallen asleep. His head lolls to one side from the ever present turtleneck collar, his glasses sit low on the bridge of his blunt, waxy nose, his mouth is lax, and his lids flutter rhythmically, as if he's dreaming of ancient fields to plow. For this ride he's adopted her own strategy for airplanes, the few times she's taken them. Maintain a comatose veneer, and the gods of aviation will smile.

So she's left with Officer Stevens, a handsome young black cop, who looks about twelve but is probably twice that. Nancy can see where he once had initials carved in his hairline. The new hair has taken on a peculiar topography. He takes out all four studs on his pierced ear when he comes to work. It's his right ear that's pierced, so he must be straight. She wonders what his girlfriend thinks of when she sees his nails, bitten down to the quick. Probably she loves him anyway, the way Carol loves Riley and Nancy loved Frank. Officer Stevens is most likely a rookie, definitely not part of the hard-core group of police who must already be up there dealing with the case. When she looks at young policemen like Officer Stevens, she thinks about their possible connection to Danny. Has any one of them ever killed a man? Certainly not Officer Stevens.

Nancy wonders sometimes about Marilyn, who may be the most lost of anyone she knows. Here she is riding back to Danny, but Marilyn will never see Eddie again. Nancy has folded Marilyn back into the story, she knows. Like something small lost in the bedsheets, she is mostly gone from Nancy's mind. But she has heard from Carol that Marilyn is back at her mother's house. She knows that the Nova house is empty. When she opened a window the other night to let in an early warm breeze off the lake, she thought of how Eddie would climb through Danny's window and suddenly just arrive. Marilyn would call many hours after Nancy expected Eddie to be missed. She and Marilyn had never discussed Frank, but Marilyn knew all along. Even so, Nancy's heart used to jump when

Marilyn's voice spoke over the phone. After all, Nancy wasn't French or suave or liberated enough not to think sometimes that Marilyn's televised accusation was true: Nancy had taken everything.

If what happened to Eddie hadn't happened, she and Frank might have met for years in bars and odd restaurants. They might have sent their kids off to college and lost some of their hearing and still spent weekends together to no one's alarm. But the world had changed, and now a whole city block stood as a memorial. Two houses could never be inhabited by the same people again. Maybe they should both be torn down, Nancy thinks, or fenced off as if the ground is cursed.

It's terrible, all the things that Nancy must lament. The pain fills her throat and makes her swallow air. She wonders what Officer Stevens sees as he sits beside her. Probably a small sad woman, nothing more monstrous. And sometimes this modest disclaimer—that she's a normal woman, a mother—is enough to let her breathe.

But as soon as she lets go of the guilt, the fear returns. It is predicated on what she can't know until it happens, what will unfold when they arrive. All she knows right now is that Frank's crazy brother ran off to his girlfriend's house, where she convinced him to call the cops. They have the woods surrounded. Both Danny and Frank have been seen in the house alive and well. What they do in there is hard to imagine. Probably life is pretty normal, like an extended version of the camping trips they took when Eddie was still alive. That's what Nancy thinks when she doesn't want to lose control.

If Frank gives up Danny with no trouble, he'll be taken without harm. She can picture her boy going one way while Frank is taken into custody. She still doesn't fully believe it's a crime to want to keep living in a way that makes sense. Sense is so relative. She's not one to judge a thing. Who can know how Frank endures this or Marilyn or Danny. Who can judge how long any of them will last. If Eddie had killed her boy, she might be dead by now. She might do something crazy involving pills or deadly speed.

So she understands why the police are concerned that Frank might be so desperate he'll try to kill himself or even hurt Danny. That's what Officer Diller told her this morning. A little apologetically, he confided that they have to be prepared for anything. He sounded as if the possibility of violence were somehow his fault, which made Nancy fear what tactics his men are willing to adopt to avoid it. She can imagine guns trained on the house already. And she's told him to be careful and to tell his men that, too. She lied once. When she told him it didn't sound right to her that Frank could have violence in mind. She won't believe that more harm may be coming their way.

She hopes it'll happen like this: they'll arrive and then the police will let her talk on a phone or a megaphone to Danny. And Frank will come out with his hands up and a sheepish grin on his face as if he's done nothing more serious than misplace someone's keys. Then Danny will race past him out of the house and she and her son will walk away together. It's that simple.

What will Nancy do when she sees Frank? That's what she can't decide. Maybe she'll just pretend he's not there, let the authorities take care of him. But with Danny there will be unaccountable joy, joy she can't name. She smiles at Officer Stevens, who offers her a shy little grin.

"How long will it be?" she asks him.

"Three or more hours if the weather holds up."

The sky, as far as she can see, is empty of clouds. May sixth is a beautiful day full of premature sunshine and warmth. With summer more than a month away, days like these are rare blessings. "If the weather holds up" must be Officer Stevens's most polite effort to ask her not to ask him. He doesn't want to take responsibility for what this ride might deliver. Or maybe it's a test of her reactions. Nancy would guess that she may be under scrutiny just like Danny and Frank in the woods.

The police are right that she may be dangerous, too. When she pictures the stock hostage version of what may happen, she sees herself running toward Frank and stripping her boy from his arms with her bare hands. Nancy will hurt Frank if she must. She sees herself going for his neck and beating on his chest with her fists, and when she imagines this, the air abandons her lungs, her ears fill with blood, and her hands clench. Nancy wonders how much of what's roiling inside her, like a late autumn storm on the lake, is observable to Officer Stevens.

"Good weather lately," she finally mutters unconvincingly, knowing she has no sense of the weather. Her weather has been the atmosphere of her front room, where she's waited by the phone for two and a half weeks for the call that finally came this morning. Her crisis phone, her nuclear winter, months of living with incomprehension, then bitter surprise, then hope.

"We've located your son," an official voice said. "He's in Wisconsin."

"He was that close?" Nancy shouted. "Why did it take you so long?" She thought of the time that Guy was right next door with Eddie while she and Danny frantically searched the neighborhood.

Less than an hour after the call, Officer Stevens pulled up in his shiny white car, and they were streaming down the interstate. It's hard to believe that they're the only ones on a mission, that their fellow travelers are heading for discount malls, mattress outlets, podiatrists, and used-car lots. Normal life takes place all around them with a composure that rarely pierces her desperation.

"Good weather," she finally agrees, but Officer Stevens doesn't seem to be listening anymore. He's squinting down the road toward one of those shiny patches that look just like water. Whenever Nancy read of oases as a child, she pictured the places on roads that glitter up and are gone.

Out of the blue, Officer Stevens asks Danny's age.

Nancy tells him that Danny just turned twelve.

He says it's a tricky age, and she agrees. Officer Stevens tells her that children are something.

Something, Nancy smiles, training her eye on the gleaming road, the bright, unreal hope that this trip will be easy.

Frank

IT SEEMED LIKE a gesture of sanity to build a fire in Ronnie's fireplace. Besides, knowing the men were waiting in the woods made Frank too jumpy to sit still, especially since the two bottles of gin that had quieted him in Ronnie's absence were gone. He stood just within the frame of the window behind a rough, yellowed shade squinting into the trees where he counted twelve, maybe fourteen figures. The men were bustling about, gathering in packs and talking to each other. They were telling O. J. Simpson jokes and drinking coffee out of thermoses and talking about some Dominican's forty-million-dollar baseball deal. Now and then Frank could hear the cracks and burps of a public address system. Now and then he heard a cough or a casual laugh. Dogs barked somewhere beyond the trees, and beyond that he could hear a train anxiously approaching a crossing. He thought when he stared very hard that he could see the valises where the men kept their rifles and sights ready to use.

Frank's nerves were raw, his head ached, his heart felt jumpy, like rumors and shadows determined its rhythm. He hadn't washed or shaved or slept a full night in four days. Some activity would soothe him. Having the boy help him place the logs in a meticulous pile would make a routine to pass the time. Maybe he'd even let Danny light the fire if he acted interested. He remembered how Eddie had always wanted to light candles, logs, or matches. That was an essential difference between sons and daughters. Daughters sat composed, waiting to grow up, while sons wanted to climb up flagpoles, jump off sheer cliffs, dance into impossible traffic, twirl with their eyes closed in the proximity of campfires. Sons dared you to let them get killed all the time.

Frank's mistake had been to take Eddie up on it. Not really, though. His mind was playing with him again, telling him lies. Frank knew he had wanted his son to live. He wasn't going to let sleepiness and nerves talk him into any other interpretation.

"Here," said Frank to the boy. "Now come and help."

"What?" Danny asked, as if he didn't understand that Frank was addressing him.

"Have you looked outside today?"

"Why?"

Frank heard no hint of knowledge in Danny's voice. "Men are out there. Come here and look," he answered.

The boy stood with him behind the window shade. Frank unveiled a crack of window out of which Danny could gape. He couldn't imagine how the boy hadn't noticed them before. Maybe their retreat into the woods had caused such numbness that the world had lost its relevance to him, too.

"The police know we're here?" Danny's voice rose with hope.

"Sure."

Tears came to Danny's eyes as Frank replied. His stomach queasy, his throat closed with apprehension, Frank turned away from the boy, then heard his voice from somewhere behind Frank's shoulder. Thinking about the men in the woods was one thing. Seeing them beyond the fragile walls that stood between him and the end of the road was another story.

Agitated with the news, Danny spoke. "So what are you going to do?"

"Make this place more cozy. After we start the fire, I'll decide. Now go get me four or five logs from that pile and a handful of sticks."

Frank watched Danny move across the room as he headed toward the pile of logs. Nothing could really keep the boy from dashing through the front door to safety if he had the nerve. Frank thought of the night of LuAnn's visit, how he had brought Danny back from the woods with the tight cuff of his hand around the boy's neck. It must have hurt, Frank realized now, as he watched the boy slumping toward him with sticks and logs and fearful eyes.

At the end of Danny's second trip to the fireplace, Frank assembled the logs into a pyramid. He remembered how small tasks like raking leaves and pruning rose bushes had once made him feel so content. He wondered if his jangled nerves could be soothed by anything short of a few more bottles of gin and the long, artificial sleep they would induce. Sleeping was out of the question with the woods full of cops. He looked toward Ronnie's spare kitchen for coffee grounds or maybe some over-looked Benzedrine from his speed freak days stashed in a drawer.

"Now take these matches. Light the sticks on top for me."

"I've never made a fire," Danny said.

"Hold the match to the sticks until they light. Try to get that first log at the same time." He hoped the fire would light quickly or he might lose his patience.

Danny took a long fireplace match out and struck it on the container bottom. It made a small flare, which seemed to surprise him. It was impossible that he had never lit a match before.

"Now hold it there just like that," Frank said impatiently as the twigs caught fire and the top log began to smoulder.

"Why are we making a fire anyway?"

"So they'll know we're safe."

"Why wouldn't we be safe?"

"Maybe they think I'll hurt you."

Frank and the boy stared into the fire for a good minute before more could be said. He wondered if it had made Danny frightened to hear him speak what the boy had probably feared all along.

"They could shoot us right now," Danny offered.

"Why would they want to shoot you?"

Danny shifted his weight tensely, eyeing Frank peripherally as he spoke. "Will my mother be coming up here?"

Frank thought how good it was that they had the fire. It provided a natural focal point, making it seem normal in its presence to speak without looking at each other. "She probably will," Frank said, careful to betray no emotion.

If Danny sensed what Frank felt now, he'd be running for cover. Losing Eddie had made the world unsafe forever. It was a reciprocal relationship. The world, for its danger to him, had made him a danger to the world. He was close to losing his composure and letting Danny see the genuinely terrifying weight of his desperation now that men were staked out in the woods and the whole world was buzzing with the news. He felt his hands shaking and folded them quickly toward his chest to still them.

"Do you still love my mother?" Danny asked shyly.

What if a man other than his own father had loved Frank's mother? What sense would he have made out of it? What if he had then stopped loving her? Or what if he had never loved her but visited her in the dead of night, touched her breasts, and entered her body, plundered her house? Frank couldn't imagine which wrong answer Danny was seeking.

"I loved her," Frank finally replied. A piece of kindling hissed and both of them listened intently, as if it were part of the discussion.

"How about your wife?" Danny asked. His voice seemed to have a little more confidence now. Frank had feared talking all along. The more he spoke, the less he controlled himself or the boy.

"I always loved my family. She was part of my family, wasn't she?"

Frank watched the boy grow very quiet and move away from him. Until then, they had been standing no more than an arm's length from each other facing the fireplace. Now Danny was nearly across the room from Frank but no closer to the door. Frank looked nervously toward the windows, which were uncovered except for the one in the front room. Maybe he should take sheets and try to drape them somehow. Ronnie probably had thumbtacks tucked away. If he could leave the house, he would get some boards and nail them over the windows, but that was out of the question.

Frank wondered if Danny had a plan or whether the boy, stunned by his captivity, experienced every moment with as much raw surprise as Frank himself did. His heart pumped noisily and his teeth felt disposed to chatter. He massaged his throat, trying to calm his pulse.

"You loved Eddie a lot," Danny said from his new distance.

"How old are you, Danny?"

"Twelve."

"How do you know so much?"

"I don't know anything, really."

"You have lots of questions."

"I'm sorry," Danny said softly. "When can I leave?"

"I know you want to get out of here, but I really can't let you go."

They stood yards apart in the quiet.

"It's hard to say why I need you," Frank continued, "but if I let you go right now, I can't imagine the rest of my life."

Frank spoke slowly and felt more anxious with each word. "It's not much of a life, but it's still something." His voice invited agreement.

"I don't understand," Danny replied.

More hissing and shifting of logs. It was remarkable really, almost absurd, how loud a fire could be. It disturbed Frank's train of thought and made him sound more emphatic than he felt. "I couldn't imagine how I'd go on living till I saw you in that park." Frank began to pace around the cabin, passing each window and pausing to stare out for a moment. Whenever he moved, it seemed the whole woods shifted and breathed in unison.

"But you hardly ever talk to me."

Frank was oddly amused by Danny's new observation. "I'm not talking about conversation."

"Then why do you need me?"

"Because."

"Because why?"

"Not because you shot Eddie."

"No?" Danny's voice was high and quivery with emotion. "Sometimes I think maybe you're going to kill me because of Eddie. I'd kind of understand if you did."

Blood pounded at Frank's temples. "That's not what I ever planned to do."

"Being stuck here, how does it help you?"

He guessed that Danny was trying to reason his way out the door. He'd lose Danny, he knew that, too. It would happen as soon as the men got tired of waiting. Frank was acquainted with lots of cops in Chicago. They had short attention spans and not too much patience about them. They wanted to take care of business, get off their shifts, and go to their second jobs or their cottages in Michigan City or their neighbors' boozy wives. He'd seen them kidney-punch suspects for taking too long just stooping to get into a squad car.

Meanwhile though, Frank wanted Danny's agreement, and it was his duty to keep talking until he got it. "I bet we think about the same things a lot, Danny," Frank finally added, feeling slightly false. "That helps me."

Frank thought of sermons, how priests can't possibly be convinced by every sincere word they utter. Still, Frank's half-truths were emptying him of his fear. He suddenly felt calm, like he could sleep a long time despite the men outside, their unintelligible noises, and the potential of their guns.

The boy paused and looked seriously at Frank and both became quiet. The men in the woods could be heard shouting something to them through the PA system they'd now gotten running. Frank looked out toward a man in a short jacket, stomach gaping, who manned the machine.

"They're asking if we're okay," Danny reported as if Frank might be deaf.

Frank felt his heart hammering out of his chest.

"They're saying our names again."

"Tell them."

"Tell them what?"

"That we're okay."

Frank knocked with his fist at a crust of brown paint on a window frame and managed to open a side window a crack.

At the top of his lungs, Danny shouted, "It's me, Danny. We're fine in here." Turning to Frank he asked, "Do you think they're going to break in?"

Frank heard the hope in Danny's voice.

"Sooner or later."

"Today?"

"Tell them I'm not armed."

"What?"

"Say I have no weapons."

"We have no weapons," Danny shouted robustly toward the woods.

They looked at each other for a long time waiting for a voice.

"I think we have a while before they get tired of waiting," Frank added.

"Will they shoot you?"

"They might." Frank paused and tasted his saliva. He thought about his blood, Eddie's blood. He thought about Nancy, the last time he had her in the firehouse. "But I don't want to think about their guns. What I want to do is walk out of this room with you. We're going to go into the basement and do some work down there."

"You and me?"

"Right."

"What are we going to do?"

"Just some digging. Maybe we can escape that way."

Danny came toward Frank and dropped to his knees on the

floor. Hugging Frank, he broke into tears. "I want to go now. I want my mom."

"Danny," Frank said with exasperation, "we're going to dig our way out and leave together." He felt breathless with this information. His chest ached, his face smarted, and his fingers throbbed and felt oddly thick. When he stooped to pull Danny up by the arm so he could twist it if he had to convince him to stay and listen, a wave of nausea cut his body loose from his feet. He faltered and grabbed at the mantle to steady himself.

"C'mon now. Let's get started while it's still light."

Still holding Danny by the wrist, he made the boy walk in front of him. Using his free hand, Frank began rearranging the furniture. Methodically he pulled every available object—a green torn love seat, a beige vinyl hassock, the kitchen table, three chairs, and a plaid dog bed in front of the door. "Now help me with this." He pointed Danny toward piles of news-papers that Ronnie stored near the fireplace.

He imagined the men with binoculars wondering what all the movement was in the house as the two entwined figures half-dragged, half-carried the six stacks of paper to the door. He remembered films where snipers pick off well-manicured men as they stand in their penthouses pouring a martini, studying their cuticles, or dialing a rotary phone. Dragging Danny toward the front window, he peered out. It was too early for them to be shooting at him. He thought of Ronnie, the war hero, trembling in the bamboo of Viet Nam. What would it be like to be gone just like that, the way a spark van-ishes from the fire, the way Eddie died in a mindless flash?

"I know it's silly," Frank said breathlessly, as he continued to waltz Danny around the front room, pausing before panes of glass, baring his face and chest toward the shooters in the woods, "to make sure all the windows are locked." Pausing long in front of the one he had opened, he dallied with it. Finally, he managed to slam it shut with his one free hand. "You know why it's silly?" he asked the boy. His eyes stung and breath came to his throat in loud wheezes.

"Because they can just break them?"

"Right," Frank grimaced. "No matter what I do, they have me, but I have to try anyway."

Nancy

NANCY HADN'T PICTURED Ronnie's house to be in such a pastoral setting, but when she and Officer Stevens pulled up, she noticed the melting snow and patches of daffodils, a tidy porch and smoke from a chimney. She had pictured a hut where Frank's brother lived, a hastily built shack where Frank held Danny hostage. It looked more like the storybook house of a country cousin or a kindly grandparent. She thought of Danny living inside its wall for two and a half weeks and tried to see through to where her son might be waiting. Would Frank keep him tied up? She doubted it. But why else wouldn't he be dashing out the door as soon as he heard the hopeful sound of wheels on the gravel?

She was just about to tell Officer Stevens that this couldn't be the right place when Riley interrupted.

"Look at the woods," he said calmly to Nancy. "It's crawling with cops." She peered away from the house toward the trees and saw men standing in random groups. Most trained their eyes on the new car that had arrived, but a few were deep in conversation. All of the men wore flak jackets. Some held walkie-talkies. A few had rifles propped near their sides like garden tools, but most of the arsenal Nancy assumed the woods contained wasn't directly apparent. Maybe the ominous trailer parked just where the trees began held weapons as well as radios, lemonade, coffee, sandwiches, decks of cards, tear gas, and rounds of ammunition.

A barrel-chested man approached her side of the sedan as soon as they had parked it near the trailer. He motioned for her to open her window as she was beginning to exit the car. Standing up weakly, she felt unbalanced, as if she was too fragile to stand on this ground. She glanced at Riley, who, feet planted firmly, was surveying the area. He should have worn something warmer than his gray, frayed raincoat, she thought to herself. She watched Riley's face as he moved his lips silently, calculating something it was impossible for her to recognize, much less name.

"What, Riley?" she asked, but the barrel-chested man had already begun talking to her.

"I'm Officer Grabek," he said. The man had mild reddish gray hair and wore a flak jacket over his large girth. Over his flak jacket was a winter-weight police parka bearing the initials of the Wisconsin State Police. Over his shoes were galoshes even though the ground was mostly dry. She noticed his hands, which were bare, small and delicate for his size.

"I'm Danny's mother." It was useless information really, so redundant that she thought she might begin to cry. "This is my friend Riley Flowers, and Officer Stevens, who brought us up here." Officer Stevens waved as he walked off to join the men near the trees. Riley was standing next to her now and took her by the arm. They could have been middle-aged parishioners on a sunny Sunday rather than participants in what the papers and news stations were calling a tense hostage drama. Nancy looked up at the sun, which felt warm on her face. The days were lengthening quickly this time of year. There were several more hours of light to work with. She felt Riley Flowers leave her side and edge toward Officer Grabek.

"He's a good man, Frank Nova is," she heard Riley say to Grabek almost as soon as they stood together. "He would never harm the boy."

"This is what we do," Officer Grabek said calmly. "We wait and hope you're right."

"It hardly seems like waiting when the woods are full of shooters," Riley said softly. "Sometimes don't you people feel a need to use all this since you've brought it along?" His hand swept the horizon and included the men, their weapons, and the tactical company trailer that sat squat and low near the trees. "Give Frank time. He'll give you the boy, I assure you."

"We hope to end this peacefully," Officer Grabek said. "It would be best for all of us if we can convince him of that."

"Have you spoken to him?" Nancy felt hesitant to say anything more, hesitant even to acknowledge the plain truth of what was happening to her and Riley and Frank and Danny and all the men in the woods. "Is my boy okay?"

"We've made some initial contact, and so far everything is stable."

"So you've seen them?" Riley asked.

"About two hours ago they were looking out of the windows and we talked over a PA system with your son."

"Her son," Riley corrected.

"We haven't seen them in a while now," Grabek continued. "They seem to have gone into another part of the house."

Why this information made Nancy feel suddenly ill she couldn't say. It was reasonable that reduced contact might signal trouble. She couldn't imagine how she would get through the next few hours or days feeling as she did. She thought of other desperate moments, the day Alex left her, that night on Marilyn's porch when she banged the door and howled and how, during Eddie's funeral, she was passed out on her kitchen floor. The fear she felt now was worse than on any occasion except the moment she'd discovered Danny under the porch. "Is it bad that they're in another part of the house?" Nancy finally asked, pleading with her eyes for an answer that might quiet her nerves.

"It's not bad," Officer Grabek replied.

"Does the house have a basement?" Riley Flowers asked.

"Yes," Grabek answered.

"That's where they are."

"How do you know that, Riley?" Nancy asked.

Before Riley could answer, several of Officer Grabek's associates approached their group. "Come with us," a tall blond policeman said. His name tag said Odalioc. Officer Grabek began to walk toward the large police van and the group followed.

The vehicle didn't look much different from the blood mobile that came to Nancy's office twice a year or the book mobile that used to visit Danny's preschool or a traveling fire safety exhibit she and Danny had once visited at a carnival. It was a sign of the times that there were precise vehicles for every emergency. There were specially packaged items called hostage kits stacked on low cabinets in the van. There were men talking to one another in quiet voices about the weather and Memorial Day. The same men would be the ones to take up weapons and shoot.

Nancy felt afraid to speak in their midst. "I just want my boy back," she said quietly as Officer Grabek explained they had hours of waiting before they'd move.

"As long as he's safe, we'll hold back," he finished.

"He'll be safe," Riley Flowers assured.

Riley Flowers had known Frank for years, well before Nancy had even met him. Riley had essentially seen Frank grow up since he and Marilyn had bought their house more than a decade ago. He and Frank used to bowl together in a church league, Riley had once told Nancy in a time not like this. Then, facts about Frank had been more like embroidery decorating the fabric of what she knew. Like any lover, she had been eager to learn all she could. Sensing her desire to know, Riley, consummate gentleman, had filled in the gaps. Several times a week he provided her with news or history of Frank. He had the good sense never to discuss Frank in Danny's presence and the discretion not to chide her eagerness to learn of her neighbor's sporting habits, career history, or minor ailments.

Officer Grabek, who had left her momentarily standing alone with Riley, returned to explain that even as they waited, his men were establishing a connection with the house. Listening devices would be activated within minutes and then they could know every move of the people he referred to as "the man" and "your son."

"Frank Nova is the man," Riley Flowers said curtly.

"We know his name," Officer Grabek smiled.

Without further conversation, Officer Grabek ushered Nancy and Riley into another room of the van, where two men in earphones sat talking softly behind monitors packed with knobs and buttons. "As soon as we have this set up, we'll hear every word they're saying wherever they are in the house," Officer Grabek explained.

"You'll be able to hear Danny's voice," Riley whispered. He squeezed Nancy's shoulder in support.

The thought made tears come to Nancy's eyes. She quickly blotted them with the sleeve of her jacket. It served no purpose to show Officer Grabek and his men how unhinged she had become. Riley put his arm around Nancy and spoke in muted tones. "Things will be fine despite these technologically advanced hooligans," he added even more softly.

Static could be heard through the monitors. Then buttons got adjusted and two voices filtered out, one of a tired man and the higher one of a child. The officers looked at Nancy, and Nancy looked at Riley in disbelief as she heard Frank say as clearly as if he were standing next to them, "My arms are killing me."

Then a smaller voice, which thrillingly belonged to her son, added, "I'm tired, too. Can we sleep in our regular beds?"

"We can't sleep at all," Frank's voice replied, "at least I can't. You lie down there with that blanket. By tomorrow we'll be all dug out."

That was all Nancy could hear. She didn't know who was speaking or what was being said around her as she repeated again and again in her head, "Can we sleep in our regular beds?" These were the simple words of her son, which somehow promised that life could once again be normal.

"He sounds fine," Riley announced to whomever might be listening.

"So far so good," Officer Grabek replied.

"Why are they digging?" Nancy asked.

"Frank thinks they can still escape," Riley offered.

The monitor was picking up some static now, but no more voices.

"Probably they're resting down there," Grabek added.

Nancy stared into Riley's eyes, hoping for more reassurance.

"I wish I could see him right now," she said.

"Soon enough," Officer Grabek assured her. "Soon as they fall asleep."

Frank

WITHOUT A HUGE amount of noise—and any noise would attract the umpteen police waiting in the woods for him to do something—how was he going to get himself out of the basement and into the car? Even if he banged from the inside on the doors, possibly jiggling the bolt, there was no way to break off a lock. He would have to use a pickax to force his way through the door if he was really set on escaping. The thought made him nearly fall asleep on his feet near where the boy still slept on the dirt floor with a blanket around him. He watched Danny for a minute as he moaned and moved and tucked his fist under his chin. To come this far and not envision better how something was blocking his way. Frank pictured the dime-store lock and remembered where the keys hung upstairs in the front room above the fireplace. They were the same keys he was going to use to open the root cellar door and place Danny inside the night the boy had run away. Why hadn't he considered that scene before he'd begun the trouble of digging all night?

Here he'd gained access through mountains of dirt to the root cellar by breaking with a sledgehammer through a cinder wall where the house joined with the mound. All night he'd spent smashing gray cinders and tar and old snow and rooty things that grew by accident and some mystery in the mix of living and man-made and accidental junk that held the house in the earth. Frank rested now, hands raw and stiff, dirt creasing bleeding double and triple blisters, soot in his mouth and nostrils, grit chafing his skin and the corners of his eyes as well.

His father had always spoken of the rewards of working with your hands. Wasn't work supposed to banish irony? Wasn't it desperation enough, the threat of being shot, to make him fully serious about the task at hand? Maybe he was so tired, punch-drunk, that it suddenly seemed funny, the futile labor he had performed so as not to have to walk out of the house through an engineered opening. Through the usual door by which people leave buildings when they're not being observed and hunted, when they haven't gone crazy and taken something not theirs to take, when they haven't stolen someone else's son.

Frank was different from Danny in this. He was digging through dirt and hiding in basements acting like some kind of senseless miner of chaos because he hadn't made this mess by accident. He had taken Danny in full knowledge, unlike Danny, who had not meant to fire the weapon. He was responsible—he was sure of that. And he continued to be responsible for himself even on this day, May the somethingth, for his actions as a man, for what he had perpetrated against Danny, only a child. Now the sheer foolishness of what he had accomplished struck him even harder and he gagged on saliva and dirt and the emptiness of what his body held.

He would need to wake up the boy just to have someone to laugh at him for this last blind effort, for all night hacking at cinder blocks and digging through dirt only to expose Ronnie's collection of canned tomatoes, the three and a half bushels of red potatoes growing eyes, the sprouting bulbs he'd never gotten around to planting, the spare parts for cars—littered here as everywhere else, the forgotten, dried-up beets left from the summer when Eddie was still alive, and the inch-wide gash of gaping sky he could observe when he pushed up on the impossible padlocked door.

He could no more break that padlock from inside than he could announce to the men that he was ready to escape with Danny and have them turn away to give him time or help him in his goal. Twice already, he'd heard their voices and not answered back and then imagined their rage at his lack of response. He knew how it tore at their chests and heightened their resolve to take him perhaps any minute.

Danny stirred behind him as Frank poked up again at the pale green door with the sledgehammer's wrong end. Maybe outside of Frank's field of vision guns pointed in his direction, a circle of men with eager fingers just waiting.

"I knew it was locked," Danny said calmly. "I knew that all along."

"Come with me," Frank said, dragging Danny to his feet and holding him again around his forearm with his own unrecognizable fist.

"What are we doing?"

"We're leaving."

"How are we going to do that?"

"We'll just walk through the door."

"I don't think the police will like that."

"They won't shoot if you're with me."

"They're not going to let you go."

"I'm doing what I'm doing," Frank said wearily. He felt as he imagined he should: bone-weary but oddly separate from himself, almost amused at what he'd become.

"It's not fair."

"What's not fair?"

"It's not fair for my mother to see this."

"How do you know she's here?"

"Didn't you hear her voice before? I heard her shout something while you were digging."

"Then she doesn't have to look."

"What if they shoot you and she has to see?"

Frank had nothing to say in response because he didn't know what he felt. Maybe that was the proper note to end on. He'd lost Eddie. Now, she could lose him in plain view. There would be some sense to that equation. Frank found something like a laugh perched near his sick smile.

"Riley's here, too," Danny added.

"How do you know that?"

"I heard him just after I heard my mom. They both said something before. It was hard to hear because of all the noise though."

Frank stood still, eyeing the piles of junk surrounding them. Some of the potatoes were blooming little green tendrils, and a shiny fender placed in a corner near the tools Ronnie stored released some light into the dim space. That Riley had come up seemed like something. In Frank's old life, the siren of an ambulance might suddenly have ended an argument he was having with Marilyn as both paused and took notice, glad their lives weren't involved in such public emergencies. So Riley's presence seemed like an answer.

"Tell them I want to talk to Riley."

"Tell the police?"

"We'll go upstairs, and you'll tell them," he smiled at the boy. What a sight he must be, dirt in his hair, caked on his lips, even his teeth, his voice sounding muffled with the stuff.

But as quickly as Frank had said he wanted to talk to Riley, the thought achieved fullness and somehow satisfied him. The desperate feeling that had filled him for weeks finally unclutched. He imagined Riley's benevolent voice and his comfortable, dour face. Shaking with fatigue, he felt an ever so slight adjustment inside himself, as if something in the world had just made room for him.

"We'll tell them they can have you if Riley comes in."

"You mean I can go?"

"If Riley comes in here."

As they walked upstairs, Danny's wrist once again circled by Frank's clenched fist, he could hear Danny's voice adjust to its better circumstance as he called to the people in the woods. "Riley, Frank says I can go if you'll see him."

They waited.

"Send out the boy, and your friend will be there," a voice burst forth from a machine outside.

"Go," Frank said, without looking at the boy. If he had to watch Danny walk through the door, he just might jump out of his skin. "Hurry up," he shouted toward him, and he felt his voice waver, adding, "Your mother's waiting." He would count to fifteen before looking outside. That way Riley would already be there or the shooter. Either was possible, Frank figured, and maybe fair.

Nancy

NANCY THINKS OF the day she had Danny so long ago it feels as if they are ancient people living a life centuries old. It happened in another world, she thinks, the day he was born. People were small and unimportant then. There were few problems that couldn't be solved, and those that couldn't would just dissipate like rain. She thinks of the painting *Peaceable Kingdom* and inserts Danny and herself in front of the animals.

All of her normal memories come into her mind dragging a fleet of regrets. Now she's a different person, one whose eyes dart everywhere, one who sniffs the air like a dog to size up the trouble. She's a scout now, she thinks, and manages, vaguely, to smile. Mostly though, her vigilance is misplaced. She's really as dumb as a stone. Things happen out of her reach. Like a child, she is simply told what will befall her next. Effortlessly, time has stretched to accommodate the inconceivable.

Now, for instance, without fully understanding why it's happening, she watches as Riley Flowers approaches Frank's brother's house, calm as a man going to market, and why shouldn't he be? That's the odd fact about life. Nothing we fear gets realized, but while we're distracted, worse things happen. Maybe one of the men with his gun trained will think of the mean thing his wife said last night over a casserole and suddenly open fire. Maybe Riley will be shot. Maybe, as in all the recent movies that flame millennial fears, a meteor will come crashing to Earth and wipe this all out.

She notices that the marksmen have their instruments ready. They are a well-trained machine. Just by looking, she can tell that not one of them takes this personally as Nancy has just imagined. I'm just doing my job, they seem to say, as their eyes peer toward the door. Every second or third shooter occasionally regards a man Nancy hadn't noticed before, a quiet, gentle-looking person who must be their leader. It follows the new logic that the leader of the SWAT team resembles a divinity student. She watches his modest black-clad arm rise from the sleeve of his flak jacket to signal something, which the men reply to by staying still and silent. They've practiced this routine, it's clear.

What trains people for life these days? What different information should she have known before leaving her home the day Danny shot Eddie? Should she have ordered her son to sit in the house all alone until she came home? Should Nancy have been equipped with a beeper so that Danny could signal that he was in trouble? The juvenile officer had suggested that. He could have beeped her before shooting Eddie then. She could have called and somehow stopped him.

For months it was part of her fear, how Alex, like an avenging angel, would swoop down from the suburbs to nab her son. But the truth was even sadder. Beyond maybe the first year, when their marriage was still breathing, Alex had never wanted Danny. Not then, when he'd been given the chance and not now. She hates how honest her mind is. It's self-betrayal to think like this constantly, examining the damage until damage is all there is.

Danny knew how to exit the house in case of fire. Danny knew how to stand in a doorway in case of a tornado. If someone had approached him and tried to give him candy, he knew not to take it. These are the lulling pieces of advice that mothers everywhere give their sons. What other words could she have spoken, she wonders as Riley disappears through the door.

This is a good day to be saved, she thinks. The sun is high in the sky, and it's cloudless, perfect. What a ridiculous thought, she realizes, as squinting, she sees nothing else but Danny. It feels hard to stand now, much less move, as he runs toward her, as she, frozen on the lawn, feels her throat grow numb and full, all at the same time. She feels herself losing her grip and tumbles toward her son. And the next thing she knows, she's on her knees on the lawn and Danny is saying, "Mom, I'm okay," in a soft crooning voice that is deeper and more mature than she remembers it being.

How can my heart stand this, she thinks as she manages, with her son's help, to pull herself to her feet. On the green, muddy lawn, they stand hand in hand like sweethearts embarking on a voyage.

Still, she feels fear and wonder. How can it be that her son is back? She looks him up and down and thinks how old he looks—maybe he's lost a little weight. And she stands behind him now and reaches her arms around his neck and holds him in front of her like that, her forehead pressed into the back of his skull, her heart hammering into his shoulder blades, then feels a great need to turn him around and look in his eyes.

They are the same eyes, she thinks, the same eyes.

About the Author

Maxine Chernoff has published five books of poetry and five books of fiction, including *Signs of Devotion*, which was a *New York Times* Notable Book of 1993, and *American Heaven*, which was nominated for the Bay Area Book Reviewers' Award in 1996. She lives in Northern California with her husband, the poet Paul Hoover, and their three children.